SPI (Spectral Paranormal Investigations)

Ghost Guardians Series, Book 2

S. Peters-Davis

Print ISBNs
Amazon Print 9780228626442
Ingram Spark 9780228626459
B&N Print 9780228626466

I0584486

Copyright 2023 by S. Peters-Davis
Cover art by Pandora Designs

* * *

Author Note: *SPI, Ghosts Guardians* series book 2 is a paranormal, New Adult, suspense romance that includes ghosts (good and evil), a touch of horror, a ghost communicator, a newly groomed detective, a few romances, and several agents of SPI (Spectral Paranormal Investigations). All of the characters, organizations, locations, and events portrayed in this novel are either products of the author's imagination or are used fictitiously.

Mature subject matter, mild sensual scenes, sensitive subject matter, and most definitely thrills

Acknowledgements

Thank you, Sharon Willett, for your critiques, edits, and encouraging comments and words.
You Rock!
Thank you, Janice, I appreciate your expertise on an excellent once over edit.
Thank you, Jude Pittman, for your continuous support and guidance. I'm forever grateful.
And thank you, Pandora Designs, for your picture-perfect creative cover.

Dedication

To those who love scary ghost stories and not so scary ones, this creates the perfect mix with a nice dollop of romance.

Table of Contents

Chapter One**Error! Bookmark not defined.**

Chapter Two.................................18

Chapter Three..............................28

Chapter Four...............................39

Chapter Five.................................52

Chapter Six 64

Chapter Seven..............................75

Chapter Eight...............................86

Chapter Nine................................96

Chapter Ten 105

Chapter Eleven 115

Chapter Twelve 125

Chapter Thirteen..........................135

Chapter Fourteen..........................147

Chapter Fifteen 159

Chapter Sixteen............................170

Chapter Seventeen 179

Chapter Eighteen 188

Chapter Nineteen..........................201

Chapter Twenty 213

Chapter Twenty-One 224

Chapter Twenty-Two 233

Epilogue....................................247

Chapter One

Bri

The creepy wailing and banging inside the more than centennial-old, three-story mansion lured me inside and up the dodgy mahogany staircase that ran along the wall to the two stories above the main floor. I hurried along the narrow hallway of the third story, passing several old-fashioned arched wooden doors, all closed. I made it to the last one. My fingers vibrated against the exterior as eerie sounds emanated from within the room. As I debated my next move, I wrapped my fingers around the ornate bronze cast doorknob, like the artifacts my gramps cherished and had stowed away for safekeeping.

"Bri Lancaster, don't you dare open that door." The urgency in Kyle's half-whispered, half-yelling voice gave me a more significant pause as he rushed down the long hallway to the end. "I'm not carrying a weapon or any other kind of protection for us."

"Do you have your smoky quartz crystal in your pocket?" I whispered as he leaned into me.

Kyle let out a sigh. "No."

I quickly pulled out the crystal I carried in my pocket and slipped it into his pocket. Then I touched the crystal dangling against my chest, a protection necklace my gramps had given me years ago that had been my grams.

Kyle drew me closer to him, grabbing my hand off the doorknob. "Why did you run all the way to the third story? The stairway is unsafe, and we haven't looked around the main floor yet." He tipped his head toward the door. "What made you stop at this room?"

"Can't you hear that?" I scrunched my nose in realization. Of course, he can't hear those sounds. After a frustrated breath, I studied Kyle. His wary expression made me step back. "Right. I expect you to hear and see as you do with SPI's paranormal equipment."

He grasped the doorknob. "I'll look inside."

I pressed my fingers over his. "No. You're not going in there without first having a way to see what's inside. The wailing and banging are so loud it should scare the neighbors who live miles from here. That is if they could filter paranormal sight and sound." Something struck the other side of the door so hard the wood should've splintered. Then nothing, as if we stood in a vacuum. My hearing went dead, and my ears refused to pop.

"What the heck?" Kyle shook his head as he tapped his ears. "Did your ears just plug?"

I nodded, staring at the door, unsure of what I expected. Kyle's hearing reacted like mine, which told me the entity in the room carried powerful energy. Prickles propelled over my arms and spine like a raging lava flow. Suddenly, my body overheated, and I felt vulnerable. Then the stench of rotten eggs hit and stole my breath. I covered my nose with the palm of my hand.

"What's wrong?" Kyle stared at me with his stormy blues.

"We gotta get out of here and come back more prepared." I yanked Kyle toward the stairway. "We need a full investigation of this place with SPI."

"What's going on, Bri? Your face is as white as snow." He stopped me. "You're trembling." His fingers squeezed mine.

"Trust me. We. Need. To leave. Now!" I jerked him by the hand until he stood beside me. "Run!"

We busted down the stairway, creating some broken steps in our wake. I couldn't breathe. The whole place suddenly reeked of death. We blew through the front doorway, not bothering to shut the door, and stumbled down the porch steps to Kyle's SUV.

What happened here?

Once inside the vehicle with the doors locked, I looked back at the house. "Wait a moment."

The mansion appeared white as if freshly painted, and every window streamed warm, welcoming light, making the snow glisten as it drifted to the ground. It looked like a peaceful, sparkly Christmas card until a sudden movement in the doorway drew my attention. A smoky shadow formed into a tall man wearing a long dark cloak. His ominous black eyes pierced and paralyzed me as he crossed his arms over his chest. Then the door slammed shut with an extreme explosion that broke through the sound barrier in my ears.

"What just happened? My ears feel like they're bleeding." Kyle's wide eyes explored my face.

"You heard that?" That entity emanated power and pure evil, strong enough that people who weren't spirit-aware would react to it.

"Hell, yes, and my ears are so sensitive right now, I could probably hear a cotton ball drop fifty miles away." Kyle started the SUV.

My hearing tuned in the same way, which made no sense. Explosions like that usually left a person deaf, at least for a while.

"I want to research this place, maybe a history of the owners. Luke's too busy, like Max, with culinary school, and their interning at your dad's restaurants has already started. I miss his techy ability." Kyle dropped the gear into reverse. "Man, it got dark fast. Wasn't the sun still shining when we arrived?"

I glanced at the glowing upstairs window. A slim woman dressed in a skimpy white dress or nightgown stood like a statue and watched us until we hit a curve in the drive. I couldn't tell what her expression portrayed or the exact century of her clothing. But I did know something horrific had happened in that house. "I think I just saw the woman Jacob Redding described when he reported a woman walking alongside this house. Do you recall reading that from the report your dad gave us?"

As Kyle swerved onto the road from the lengthy driveway, I saw a plaque with a naked woman and a snake curled around her body and written at the bottom was 'established 1885.' I didn't see it when we arrived, and it vanished as we drove past.

Kyle lifted and squeezed my hand. "I'll talk to Dad again to better understand what that snowmobiler found here. Dad assigned me to this investigation under the impression it might be something for SPI. His initial thought was trespassing kids. I didn't see any evidence of that inside or outside the front of the building. I never saw any snowmobile tracks, for that matter. Too much snow fell and is still falling." Kyle's fingers slipped from mine. He gripped the steering wheel with both hands as he pulled onto the narrow road and then slowed for a deer crossing in front of us. The headlights picked up a second deer trailing the first.

"Well, that mansion is jam-packed with paranormal activity and not the easy kind. I've never felt such vile hostility. That place seemed filled with something evil, and there's at least one woman and a demonic-looking man inside."

"Tell me more about the woman and the man."

"The woman appeared slender, dressed in a nightgown from most likely late 1800s. She stood at the upstairs window when we backed down the driveway." I could only imagine why and none of my thoughts came with good tidings. "I got the impression that she's trapped there." Then I explained how the mansion changed before I saw the scary man at the front door and mentioned with detail the disappearing sign at the driveway and road junction.

"Wow, this sounds like some of the horrific ghost stories I heard as a kid. You know, sort of like Jack the Ripper kind of stuff. That mansion might be the place a lot of kids visited for kicks and scare-dom, although I saw no sign of it today. In my teens, I never got that hype and didn't join in the haunted house experiences. Well, until I met James and Sandy Wyant and became a member of their SPI business." He glanced my way, cracked a smile, and then concentrated on the snow-covered road.

"I can't believe how busy SPI has become since Luke listed them on several websites. I'm always working outside the office now."

I smiled when Kyle glanced at me. "I think Sandy is considering another person to help with my accounting work, so I'm free for traveling."

"I can finally use my investigation skills and close some of the Kalamazoo County Police Department cold cases and SPI's cases. Who knows, maybe I'll be traveling with you if the places we investigate are in Kalamazoo County." Another deer darted in front of the car. Kyle stomped on the brake pedal and skidded, stopping just off the edge of the road. Heavy snow continued to fall and stuck to the windshield, challenging the wipers. "Well, hell, that didn't go so well." Kyle let out a deep breath and shifted the SUV into park.

The headlights picked up thick flakes, shifting and sprinting past, but beyond those lights, I couldn't see squat. "The wind just picked up like a terrifying thriller..."

"Now you're sounding like Max and Luke's banter." He chuckled and then sobered. "I don't know about any storm warnings, but we'll get some drifting for sure and stuck if we don't keep going. It's typical for January Michigan weather." Kyle reversed and slowly got the car back on the road. "Look at how much snow already covers the road. I wouldn't be able to tell where the road was if not for the trees."

After a few miles, I pulled off my safety belt and moved to the forward edge of the seat, peering out the front window. "Go slow.

We don't want to drive off the road. This stretch is full of curves, and the trees are farther away from the road, harder to see the edge with all the accumulating snow." I strained to see through the curtain of snowflakes. Then the headlights picked up a slender young woman in a thin, white nightgown. She stood in front of the SUV. "Stop!" I yelled.

Kyle slammed on the brakes. The SUV skidded helter-skelter over the woman as I closed my eyes.

When the vehicle finally stopped, I jumped out and ran to the back, following the tire tracks as best as possible. "Kyle, bring a flashlight."

"Bri, what did you see? What are you after?" A beam of light bounced along with the falling snow until it captured my face.

"Kyle, you ran over a woman." I turned away from the blinding light.

He grabbed my arm and spun me toward him. "I didn't see a woman. We would have heard and felt something if we drove over a person. I didn't, did you?"

That took me back to the moment. "I saw a woman. She wore something similar to what the woman in the window had worn, only the female in the window had long dark hair, and the one in the road had blonde." I grabbed the flashlight out of Kyle's hands and waved the beam over the tire tracks. Nothing. I rarely made the mistake of misidentifying a spirit for a live person.

"Perhaps the mansion and the evil within it threw off my sensitivity ability."

Kyle pulled me tight against his body. "By the sounds of it, I think there's a doozy of a paranormal event happening. I will mark this spot, and I want you to get back inside the SUV." He walked me to the passenger door that I'd left open. "Get inside. I'll find some branches for the marker, but that might take me a few minutes."

I climbed in, realizing too late I still held the flashlight. Kyle trudged through the deepening snow until I couldn't see him or the light from his cell phone he thankfully carried. We had driven several miles from the mansion, and to see a spirit this far from there dressed similarly to the one inside the place, meant she was stuck here for a reason. I recalled Martin and Gloria's ghosts were attached to the vehicle where they'd died. Their bones had gotten buried in the woods not far from the car. I sensed the two women I'd seen were connected somehow, and it would take some investigation to figure out the who, how, and why.

A snowball smashed against the passenger window and startled the crap out of me. I couldn't see out the window through the caked snow. A gloved hand swiped the frozen stuff aside, and Kyle grinned at me. His cheeks looked bright red with ice coating his eyelashes as steam puffed from his mouth. I signaled for him to get inside.

Kyle walked like a frozen zombie around the vehicle until he climbed into the driver's side. He immediately removed his gloves and shoved his hands over the defrost vent. "Dang, it's cold out there. I managed to find some long branches and build a teepee-looking marker to show where you saw the woman." He settled back and fastened his safety belt. "I also marked this location on my cell phone map, so we know when we're close to my marker in case the snow buries it." He revved the motor as he wiggled his brows at me. "Buckle up, buttercup. You might be in for the ride of your life."

"Show off." I appreciated his sense of humor, but it didn't eliminate the imminent doom lurking inside that old mansion, the surrounding forest, or the long drive home. "We drove over an hour to that mansion, right?"

"Yes. This case will require research and a meeting before we head back there. We need the age of the house and a list of everyone that lived there. If we're lucky, we'll also find some of the occupants' history."

"Maybe I can still get Luke involved. He's pretty fast on his research." I pulled my cell phone out of the cupholder.

"I'm getting a lot better with digging deep on the internet, little missy. Give me a chance to prove myself and let Luke and Max stay busy with their culinary training." Kyle grinned at me, then sobered, noticing the snowy windshield. He glanced toward his watch. "It's going to take forever getting home in the dark on this path-for-a-road during snowstorm conditions."

My mind whirled, thinking of those two women and the horrific man who stood in the doorway as if guarding the entry. My brain dove into search mode for some empathic clue of what came next. "I wonder if James and Sandy ever had to deal with such malice."

"Knowing those two, they've had some experience. Although all of the times I helped out, it never felt that real to me, until you became involved. You give a play-by-play, if not during the big event, then afterward, so everyone got an understanding of what to expect next time." Kyle slammed on the brakes again. The SUV slid sideways across the road and bucked a drift that stopped us as a herd of deer bounded through the headlight beams.

"Looks like we're watching a wildlife documentary." I turned to stare out the passenger window, and another woman with long, flowing dark hair, wearing the familiar white garb, stood half-in, half-out of the vehicle.

Her glowing eyes captured mine. "Stay away," she whispered and then disappeared.

Chapter Two

Bri

"If Dad's lights are on, let's stop before we go to our place. We need to know more about that old mansion, and so does Dad." Kyle pulled into the driveway. Thankfully, lights blazed through the windows on a Monday night at ten-thirty. "Don't hold back telling him all you saw, Bri." We climbed out of the SUV and rushed up the porch steps.

Kyle used the key to his parent's house and unlocked the door.

Miles stood inside the kitchen wearing his coat and gloves, and concern etched his face. "What happened? Are you both okay? I was just leaving to look for you. Apparently, my calls weren't going through to either of you."

"We're fine but a bit rattled." Kyle glanced at me and then back at his father. "Sorry for the late visit, but I wanted you to hear what happened firsthand. Let's sit at the kitchen table." Kyle grabbed my hand and pulled me to a chair.

Miles shook his head as he pulled off his outside gear and settled into a chair across from Kyle and me. "I had no idea the weather would turn into a snowstorm, more like a blizzard. It took some time for you to get back here, didn't it?" Without waiting for an answer, he continued, "Sorry about that. Glad you made it without incident."

"Well, about that..." Kyle nodded toward me. "Tell Dad everything."

I did, not leaving out the woman in the window or the scary-looking man in the mansion doorway, or how the appearance of the building went back in time to brand new. Nor did I skip describing the sign I saw that disappeared or the distance we'd driven when we saw the last two women and how something must be keeping them stuck there.

"Wow, I had no idea that kind of history was attached to the old mansion. It makes me think of the bordello stories my grandparents shared. Turned out more of a horror story." Miles stared at me. "Did you open doors to any of the rooms upstairs?"

"None. The vibe came across as pure evil." A chill zipped up my spine like a sawblade, making me shiver, and my eyes slammed shut. Everything went dark.

Then suddenly, I popped back to the mansion, reliving each moment there. Only this time, my trip ended with me standing in front of the black-eyed man at the door. His arms reached toward me. My paralyzed body couldn't move as he grabbed my shoulders with stabbing force. I said, "I have no fear," repeating the mantra. His mouth stretched open, long and wide, and his pointed teeth lengthened. The familiar stench coated my face, the same as my earlier visit. Then I said, "I am filled with love and light; the Divine is my shield." Before I could repeat the mantra, his mouth closed, and he vanished into a cloud of black smoke.

Voices called my name, echoing inside my brain until I forced my eyes open to Kyle's handsome face. His warm hands released each side of my head.

"What happened to you? It's like you passed out in the chair, then after a bit, you're repeating a mantra. Dad and I hollered your name, but you couldn't hear us." Kyle studied my face. "You did pass out, didn't you?"

"I've never experienced anything like what just happened. I'm not sure how it happened, but I returned to the mansion and got a good picture of that man's appearance. I believe his clothing dates back to that of the 1885 plaque. That's a starting point for research of when the place was built and who owned it." My heart beat like a mountain of drums in my chest. "Some horrific trauma must have happened to that man to make him so vile. He wanted to hurt me, maybe even kill me."

"Kill you? Why?" Kyle pulled me from the chair and into his arms. "Your face went pale, like when we stood in front of that upstairs door. Maybe you need to do the same things you did with that school of kid spirits. You know. How you used gemstones to absorb all the negative energy." Kyle hugged me tighter. "Remember?"

"Of course, I remember. But I'm not sure anything can touch such a malicious man. And we don't have Gloria, Ileana, or Martin's spirits to lead the man and those women into the light. I wouldn't trust that man to be around any light soul." I didn't close my eyes for fear I'd call him to me again. The fear mantra helped me get back my courage. But those teeth and his spreading mouth reminded me of a horror movie, and I wouldn't want anyone exposed to that kind of evil danger. "I'd like to get home and research. Maybe we'll get lucky and pull up a few articles or old tales that might have something we can use."

Miles slid his chair away from the table. "I think both of you should sleep on it tonight and get a fresh start in the morning. From what you've told me, it sounds like an SPI investigation." Miles looked at Kyle. "Son, you have the reins on this one, but if you need backup from the KCPD, don't hesitate to call." He walked us to the SUV. "I don't pretend to know all of your abilities, Bri, but I know you're genuine in your capabilities at giving justice to the dead. Don't put yourself in danger, however. Promise me you won't do that." Miles touched my shoulder before I climbed into Kyle's vehicle. "Your ghost reminds me of a malevolent poltergeist the KCPD tried to eliminate years ago. Not sure who came to the rescue, but we couldn't fix that problem. Please be careful."

"I can promise you I'll figure out how to deal with this entity." That seemed the best promise I could make to Kyle's father. And to myself, I added that Kyle would remain safe no matter what happened.

* * *

"Looks like Max and Luke are already in bed. I don't see any lights on inside." Drifted snow covered most of the tire tracks from their vehicles, leading into one of the two double garage doors. "After living here for four months, I'm still getting used to this amazing house."

"Me too. I still can't believe we bought it at such a good price, and with the four of us splitting the monthly bill, we can all afford it." The layout of the place was close to the same as my parents' home, and we figured the same construction company had built it. I glanced at Kyle. "Just a heads up, I can't close my eyes now."

Kyle's gaze remained on the opening garage door as if he hadn't heard me. He parked the SUV, and we quietly made our way through the house to our bedroom, which was more like a suite. The room was huge, with a good-sized bathroom and walk-in closet. Luke and Max had the same sized bedroom, bathroom, and closet on the lower level, located at the opposite end of the house. So far, we all seemed to get along incredibly and shared the responsibility of cleaning, cooking, and outdoor chores.

I sat on the edge of the bed, wanting something to occupy my mind. Anything other than closing my eyes. I needed to research, but intuition yanked my chain away from opening that can of worms tonight. I glanced at the bedside clock. *Almost midnight, the witching hour.* I did not want to fall asleep.

Kyle walked out of the bathroom in his underwear. His ripped body stole my breath, as did his husky voice when he asked, "How come your not in your skimpy little nighty?" His eyelids dropped half-mast, and his right brow rose in what I called the *steamy sex-pot smolder.*

Burning snaps of electric charges whipped through my body, sending messages to all my lady parts, and putting ideas in my head. "You, my dear, are exactly the distraction I need right now. Perfect timing."

Kyle pulled me off the bed, wrapping his arms around me as he gently kissed me. He continued kissing my lips, face, and body with growing fervor while undressing me. When I stood in my underwear, he whispered, "Let's get under the covers, where it's warm...and I can have my way with you."

No objections on my part, and he did have his way with me, with lots of cuddling, fondling, and other things. Then I had my way with him, lasting until the wee hours of the morning.

* * *

The smell of coffee woke me. Kyle stood beside the bed, fully dressed, and held a steaming cup. "Here you go, Snickers. Mostly milk with a shot of coffee." He grinned.

"That's Gramps' name for me." I eyed him and then stared at the cup he held. "But you get a pass for using it because I want what's in your hand."

"I was going to run into the station this morning to see if I can contact Jacob Redding and hear his story firsthand, but Dad called and told me to stay home. He's also at home. I called James, and he said to go ahead and start your research here because the road to their place won't be plowed for hours, if at all. Might as well stay home today."

"Did you tell James what happened at the mansion?"

"Dad already called James about it this morning. He wants SPI as the major part of the mansion case with me as the investigative detective." He set the cup on the nightstand, drawing my attention to the clock.

"Holy Hell! It's already nine-thirty. Why didn't you wake me?" I piled out of bed, snapping the sheets and bedspread into place, then swallowing a big swig of coffee as realization hit me. *I stood completely naked.*

Kyle wiggled his brows. "You needed to restore yourself after last night, you vixen...catch up on your sleep before the research." He grabbed my arm before I made it to the bathroom door. "Where did you learn all those sexy things you did to me? Maybe I need some lessons."

"Intuition, babe. You, my dear, are my only intimate relationship." I snickered.

"Really..."

"And you don't need lessons. You know what turns me on very well, and you handle my needs like a pro."

He grinned again, wider. "Want to do it again before I leave?"

I rolled my eyes. "It's already nine-thirty. We are both late, and besides, Luke and Max are here."

"Nope, they aren't. They left together early for culinary school."

I ran into the shower. "Don't even think about it."

He didn't. He undressed and joined me in the shower, having his way with me again. *What a way to start the day.*

* * *

Kyle was on the phone when I walked out dressed and ready for the day. I poured myself another shot of coffee and added the milk, then microwaved it to perfection. I went to the desk in our sunroom, which stood next to a window with a lake view. The snow glistened from the sunlight, making the lake appear magical. We resided on the south side of Howard Lake, so the sunrise cast rays the same as the sunset but not in our faces. Luke had left a note for me that Kyle forgot to mention. He'd written several website links for the mansion research and its history of occupants. I hoped for results, so I got right down to serious research.

"Hey, sunshine, finding anything?" Kyle came up behind me and leaned over my shoulder.

"Just got started, but this first website looks promising. Pictures of old maps show bordello locations. Your dad was onto something with the bordello info from his grandfather. Who knew? This side of Michigan looks like a hideaway hot spot for some lady bliss while prestigious men traveled between Detroit and Chicago."

"Really? Wow. Print some of those maps and any info you feel is relevant. Maybe you can send some of those links to James also." He kissed the top of my head. "Looks like I'm staying home, too, at least for now. Dad's plowing his driveway and told me most roads haven't gotten plowed. I hope Luke and Max made it to culinary school all right."

"Well, Max has that giant truck with four-wheel drive." I glanced out the window, realizing clouds had pilfered the sun and were now spitting snow. It whirled in gusts of wind across the lake, and the snow seemed to increase as I watched.

"Yea, that's what they drove. Luke's little car is still in the garage." Kyle moved to a window and stared outside. "Yea, maybe I should shovel some snow before I call Jacob. Dad gave me his number."

"No." I never say 'no' to Kyle, and his wide-eyed, raised eyebrows portrayed surprise. "You should call Jacob first in case his info can help with the research."

"Good idea." He nodded, brows scrunching together as he turned and walked out.

Did I say a bad thing or a good thing? Hard to tell, so I went on with my internet investigation.

Chapter Three

Bri

I couldn't believe what I found on the links Luke had left for me. I checked out the Public Library in Kalamazoo for the year 1885. Microfilms in the lower level had maps and newspapers for that era. Hopefully, Luke would find lots of information. I hurriedly texted him, asking if he'd have time to stop and check it out after his culinary class. I knew Luke had a library membership card and was already savvy with the layout of the building. He would uncover as much as possible for a good foundation of information.

In the meantime, I opened Grams' journal to refresh my knowledge from her in-depth info on hostile, malevolent spirits. I went to the last pages and got lost in time, making notes on the different ways of eliminating negative, evil apparitions. She must have dealt with them even though Gramps didn't know much about Grams' actions with such entities.

"Hey!" Kyle plopped into the chair beside the desk.

I peeked at my cell phone, checking the time, and a whole hour had passed.

"I just got off the phone with Jacob. Do you want to hear what he had to say?" His playful smile and nodding head gave me a heightened feeling he'd learned something unique.

"Okay, shoot." I turned to face him, gently placing Grams' journal aside. "Tell me everything."

"Jacob mentioned he'd never driven his snowmobile near the mansion. He didn't know the place existed nor how he got there, and it took him forever to find his way home afterward. Apparently, the night he drove out there, the weather was similar to ours last night." Kyle studied his notes.

I glanced outside at the curtain of thick snowflakes dropping to the ground. A Cardinal struck the window, hard and fast, startling us. It sounded like a gunshot. The bird stuck to the pane for a moment as its head turned with searching eyes, making contact with me and then Kyle, who jumped up beside me. The bird's eyes closed as his bright red body slid off the glass.

"What the hell?" Kyle moved to the window and looked down. "Did you see that thing look at us? I don't see the bird. It should be lying right on top of the snow."

I moved to look and didn't see it either, nor did I see any marks in the snow. "My grams and gramps told us whenever we see a Cardinal, it's someone we knew and loved, visiting us from Heaven."

Kyle tilted his head. "Never heard that one before. And if it were true, who would do that? I mean, throw themself against a window?"

"Not sure who would knock themself out in a visit." I sighed, but on the inside, I wondered if it held a message for us. It definitely got our attention. The bird's eyes found us before it fell and vanished. That said something, and I would know sooner or later what. "Finish the conversation with Jacob."

Kyle dropped into his chair again, and I sat in mine.

"Jacob saw more than one woman outside, like ten or so," Kyle stated. "All were dressed the same, as if they were members of a club or cult, wearing white dresses, like old-fashioned sleepwear. They ran around the backside of the mansion. He thought they were in trouble and needed help. Some ran around in the surrounding forest as if to hide. And all of them disappeared before he could reach them."

"Jacob saw them?" I studied Kyle, whose mouth dropped open, but his eyes sparkled. "Kyle, that means he can see spirits."

"Yes, it does...and I wondered how long it would take you to tell me that." He grinned. "And, yes, I've already asked him to join SPI. James will meet with him later today if the roads get cleared. Although, it doesn't look like the snow will stop." We looked toward the window at a white-out of snow. "Guess Dad gave Jacob's phone number to James. So, tell me, how's your research going?"

"Well, hopefully, Luke won't hate me. I texted him to stop at the Public Library in Kalamazoo before he came home. I asked him to look up a county map for the late 1800s and also to look up any newspaper info about the mansion and the people that lived there." My belly growled so loud Kyle heard it and grinned.

"It's past lunchtime. Let's go build us a sandwich." Kyle clasped my hand and pulled me up from the chair, turning me toward the doorway into the kitchen. "After you, my dove."

I laughed hard. "My dove? Okay, my prince charming, lead the way." I yanked him around me and shoved him forward.

Then he laughed, and everything felt right in my world.

* * *

Sandy Wyant, from SPI, called me about five o'clock asking if I'd made any progress on the mansion case. I gave her everything I knew, which didn't seem like much. I even shared my blackout scenario that happened at Kyle's dad's house afterward.

"Wow, Bri, this sounds like a major case for us." I heard Sandy shuffling some papers, then she said, "I understand Jacob Redding might be joining our team. He can see spirits like you, which is excellent news. We're excited someone else can replace Max or Luke when they're unavailable."

"Yes, I'm excited to meet Jacob and discuss his ability. I don't know anyone that grew up seeing ghosts, although many people can."

"You are the first member of SPI that can see spirits, Bri. If Jacob joins our business, would you be interested in training him? James can take care of some training, but with your gifts, we could definitely use another like you. Someone that knows the exact mantra to use and the extra care necessary to keep the whole team safe."

"Who knows? I'm sure Jacob will also have things he can teach me." I moved back to the desk and pulled out a pen and paper. "Do you know his address and phone number?"

"Doesn't Kyle know that?"

"Probably, but Kyle plowed out the driveway and then drove over to his dad's, about a mile away from our house. That happened several hours ago, and I haven't heard back from him, so they probably drove to work. He thought they'd discover more information about the mansion from the old archived files in the lower levels at the police station."

"James is plowing out our long driveway right now." Sandy shuffled through some papers again and gave me Jacob's information. "If you can't make it in tomorrow, don't worry about it. I'm sure there's a lot of research required for the mansion. We'd want everything you can find on it before we make our first visit. Bri, you are so appreciated."

Her gratitude made me smile. "Sandy, you and James are also appreciated. Thank you for opening a spot for me at SPI."

"You're well worth it to us, Bri. Talk to you again in the morning so we can catch up on any other news you find." With that, Sandy hung up.

Luke's text came in on my phone: 'You are not going to believe all I found about that mansion. I wrote a ton of notes because I couldn't take the microfilm or the old newspapers out of the library. I'll send you the pictures I took with my phone of newspaper articles and my notes. Max and I are staying in Kazoo tonight due to the weather. Stay home and work. Love ya.'

Several photos of newspaper articles came through from Luke, and I couldn't wait to read them.

* * *

Kyle

After I arrived at Dad's, I drove him to work. So, I stayed at the police station, worked on my detective training, and searched for the mansion case file. At about

34

six o'clock, we drove back to my parent's place.

When we stopped in his driveway, something furry, black and white, lay next to my parent's back steps.

"What the hell is that?" Dad quickly climbed out of the SUV and ran toward the house.

"Hey, it's black and white, be careful," I yelled, sure the thing was a skunk. I hurried toward Dad. When I got close, my heart cracked in two. "Oh my gosh, that dog doesn't look a year old. What the heck is it doing outside on such a cold day?"

"Well, the pup's a male and shaking so hard I'm not sure I'll be able to stop it." Dad grabbed the dog and wrapped his arms around it. "He should weigh more than he does." Dad lifted him up and down as if defining his actual weight. "Maybe eight to ten pounds more. Are you and Bri looking for a roommate? The two of you can fatten him up."

"Someone is going to miss this guy." The pup stared up at me as if waiting for my response. Dang. Now my heart melted. How could I not take him home?

"Nope, don't think so. This guy doesn't have a collar and is way too thin and all alone, which tells me someone either dropped him here or he ran away a while ago." Dad's lips pressed together as he examined the animal. "He may have also been abused. I see some scarring. How can people be so irresponsible?" He held the puppy toward me. "Take him to Bri and see what she says."

The pup kept staring at me, almost eerily, yet adoring, if that makes sense. "Come on, little dude. You might get lucky with Bri." I already knew he had me wrapped around his little paw.

When I got inside the SUV, I whipped off my coat, covering the shivering pup. The dog, lengthier than I first thought, settled on my lap. I drove the mile home, and our driveway looked like Dad's, covered with several inches of new snow as if I'd never shoveled. My SUV wasn't as high as Max's truck, but it had four-wheel drive. I hit the button to raise the garage door and drove inside without a problem.

I grabbed the pup and hurried into the house. We found Bri in full concentration mode on the couch, snuggled in a blanket with her laptop and a notebook. When I stopped in front of her, she looked up, eyes popping wide.

"What do you have there?" She closed the laptop, set her notebook aside, and stepped over to check out the puppy. "Oh, my gosh, he's young and so cold and skinny." She lifted him out of my arms and then walked back to the couch for the blanket, wrapping it around the furry guy and handing my coat to me before she sat. Her face brightened as she studied the hairy beast. "I love him already. Where did you find him?"

"Snuggled against the back steps of my parent's house. Dad thought he might make a good roommate for us and said I might get lucky with you agreeing." I moved to the other side of Bri and slid in next to her.

"This guy was lucky you found him. We should name him, 'Lucky.'" Her hands smoothed over his fur. "I can feel his bones. His black and white scruffy fur makes him look handsome. It's soft yet wiry and curly, but he requires a good brushing."

"So that means we're keeping him?" I had always wanted a dog, but Mom and Dad thought our family was too busy to raise one.

"Yes. Now, this is a gift from Heaven." She cooed and smiled, hugging the little creature closer.

Watching her lit something inside me that thawed the cold I'd felt since spending most of the day in the cool basement of the KCPD headquarters. "You're a natural, Bri." My stomach growled. "Did you eat supper yet? I'm starving. I bet our pup is also."

"Nope. Thought I'd wait for you." Bri reached over the mutt and flipped open her laptop. "I'm going to look up what we can feed this guy until we can get to the store for some puppy food."

"Okay, that sounds like a good plan. You sit with Lucky, and I'll fix us something. Holler when you find something that I can fix for Lucky."

* * *

Bri

I found an article on the internet about feeding sick or starving dogs. I read not to give him much because he might turn glutton and over-eat, especially if he's over-hungry. We could boil chicken breasts and cut them up to get something in his stomach. Kyle cooked the two breasts we'd bought the day before while he put something else together for our dinner.

I closed my laptop and pushed it away. "Lucky, you look like an angel sent from Heaven." I snuggled him to me, and he suddenly raised his head. He stared at me with such adoration, eyes meeting eyes. "I've already fallen in love with you, sweetie."

"I love you, too, and have waited so long to make this trip to the earth realm," Grams' voice reverberated through my brain.

"Grams? Is that you inside our Lucky?" My heart pounded hard and warmth filled every inch of my insides.

The puppy's lips didn't move, but his eyes stayed on my face as my brain picked up Grams' familiar voice again, "Yes, I took the first little something available to me, which bombed out when the Cardinal hit your window. Next up was this little four-legged starvin' Marvin. Thank goodness your significant other, and his father, found me

38

before I perished a second time in my attempt to get to you."

I held Grams closer, kissing the top of Lucky's head. "I'm so glad you're here. You've arrived just in time to help us with a malicious entity, holding at least ten women hostages since the late 1800s."

"That, my dear, is exactly why I've come and wish to stay." The pup snuggled closer.

Kyle walked into the living room, carrying a tray of sloppy joes, chips, a couple of sodas, and a little dish for Lucky. "I thought you were on the phone. Who are you talking to? The pup?"

"As a matter of fact, yes."

Chapter Four

Bri

Kyle and I ate, and so did Lucky, fast and furiously. Kyle took Lucky outside to do his business, using a rope for a leash. As soon as they came back in, Lucky ran into the living room. I plopped him on the couch beside me. The pup's shivering had subsided after he'd eaten, but we'd wrapped him in a blanket anyway. He instantly fell asleep, and apparently, Grams had slept also. I would need to ask her about that, where she goes to sleep, and exactly how she can stay in the earth realm. Martin and Gloria's spirits had attached to an old car, a child and a nanny had attached to an old house, and a group of children got stuck inside an old school building. Maybe, residing in something alive kept Grams earthbound. I wanted to know how she got here.

"So, what's next?" Kyle returned to the room after taking the dishes out to the kitchen. He sat on the couch beside the puppy and me.

"I have so much research to finish. Luke sent me some pictures of newspaper articles and photographs from 1885 and a few years after. I haven't read any of it yet." I still had to tell Kyle about Grams but sensed it might be a lot to comprehend. "I need to download those pics onto my laptop for easier studying and highlighting."

"Want me to move, Lucky?"

"No, he's fine for now. There's something I have to tell you about Lucky." My heart thundered, and my face heated at the possibility Kyle wouldn't believe me. "I wasn't talking to the puppy when you came out of the kitchen." He turned toward me and studied my face. I continued, "He has another soul residing inside him, my grams."

Kyle's left brow lifted. "What are you talking about?"

"Grams wanted to come to the earth realm to help us with the evil entity at the mansion. Sounds like she's kept tabs on us." I glanced at Kyle, who was totally focused on the puppy. I sensed his avoidance to look at me was intentional. "Grams first came as the Cardinal that crashed into our window, but it died. So, she entered, Lucky, fearing the worst when no one had found him, and then you and your dad came along."

Kyle's silence and his tight-mouthed expression blared louder than any crack of thunder. He shook his head and then lifted his face to stare at me.

"Please, tell me what you're thinking." A feeling of doom thrashed my insides, making my stomach want to erupt. Had I shared too much? I thought we were passed the

41

unbelieving, although, this was a little different than seeing a ghost.

Finally, he closed his eyes and took a good long breath. Moments later, wide-eyed and tense-jawed, he said, "I did not know souls returned. Are you telling me Logan could come back?"

"I didn't realize souls returned either, Kyle. But I'm sure Grams will explain how that happened to her. She's as exhausted as the pup and probably won't awaken for hours. I'm sorry that I don't know about your brother." His face turned solemn, and again, he closed his eyes. My heart painfully expanded, like the lump in my throat. Tears welled, threatening to release as I waited for Kyle to respond.

When he finally opened his lids, he said, "Bri, I trust what you say, but I'm finding it difficult to accept." Those magnificent blues pierced me with his truth.

"Me too. But it's Grams' voice that my brain transmits as if she's sitting next to me. Grams told me why she's back, and I believe her. We need her help. I need her help." I slid off the couch onto my knees, pushed the coffee table away, and then moved in front of Kyle, parting his legs to snuggle in closer. "I feel different about this entity, more so than any other we've come across with SPI. My intuition tells me this thing can kill. I'm not afraid for myself but for everyone else that will help us deal with it. The extreme negativity in that mansion paralyzed me completely when I was at your dad's house. I've never had anything like that happen to me before...nothing has ever followed me and gotten inside my head as that thing did."

Kyle drew me up against his warmth, arms holding me so close his heartbeat merged with mine. "I apologize for questioning you. By now, I should know better." His hot breath fluttered my hair as he spoke, shooting tingles down my spine. He kissed my forehead. "I love you, Bri Lancaster. I intend to marry you someday." He tilted my head upward, and his lips met mine in a gentle, mesmerizingly slow kiss.

He wants to marry me.

Grams' voice entered my head. "If that's a proposal, you better say yes."

I went speechless.

"Well?" he said, one brow raised. When I didn't say anything because my mind turned to mush, he added, "What are your thoughts on getting married?" His brilliant blues held such promise, love, and respect, making me feel like we were in a dream. "I'm serious," he added with a hint of frustration. "I want you as my wife. And honestly, I knew that the moment I first met you in the twelfth grade."

"Really?" So strange because I had hoped Kyle would come back from college still a single man, and thankfully, he did.

"Ask Max. All I thought about was you at college, hoping you hadn't found someone else."

I smiled, knowing no one else could make me happier than Kyle. I kissed him, forcing my tongue through his closed teeth to explore for a moment. Then I pulled back for a second, kissing the corners of his mouth. "I love you, Kyle Benson," I whispered against his lips. "Will you marry me someday? That's my answer to your question about getting married, and I'm sticking to it."

Kyle chuckled. "Well, okay then. After we get done with this case, shall we make plans?"

"I think we should keep it very simple. Only immediate family and Luke can be my maid of honor, and Max can be your best man. Maybe a little ceremony out by the lake...someday? Sound good?"

"Sounds perfect." Let's seal it with a nice hot shower while our little dude sleeps." He lifted me off to the side and picked up the sleeping pup, careful not to wake him. "Come on, bride-to-be," he whispered, "I've got the perfect box Lucky can sleep in while you and I find a way we can physically seal our deal."

Of course, I followed.

* * *

Kyle carried me to bed after our romp in the shower. He checked on Lucky while I slipped under the covers. When he climbed into bed, I slid tightly against his back, stroking him into oblivion, which satiated both of us. My whole body seemed struck by lightning, entrancing all parts of me like streaming magic, until I finally fell asleep, glued skin to skin with my husband-to-be…someday.

I awoke to Lucky whimpering, so I slipped out of bed and stepped over to his box. "What's going on, mister?" I whispered. "Come here, little man." I lifted him out with his blanket and grabbed my robe from behind the bathroom door, draping it over me as I walked out of the bedroom. The living room had a lot of electronics, like a television and sound system, internet routers, and other things giving off enough spots of light that we could walk in the dark and never trip.

We settled on the living room couch. My phone lying on the coffee table read four o'clock in the morning, but I felt wide awake. I clicked the lamp for a low-level light. "Okay, Lucky. I'm going to give you a quick bath in the tub, and then we'll research veterinarians in the area. See if we can get you an appointment today, and then figure out what you can eat this morning. I have to get dressed before taking you outside to potty." Lucky stood but remained on the couch.

"Bri," Grams' voice came through loud and clear, "let's talk about that situation with Leonard Whitenmeyer, a surgeon ahead of his time until he meandered into the dark side." Lucky tilted his head, staring at me as if expecting me to acknowledge. He settled back down on his blanket, continuing to look at me.

"Okay, I'll bite. Who is Leonard Whitenmeyer, besides a surgeon gone dark? What does he have to do with..."

The dog panted, and a short yip erupted, quick yet gentle, as if to stop me from talking. "That's the 1885 name of the mansion owner. The monster who kept those women captive so they could be used and abused by men of a certain class," Grams stated, talking inside my head. "We can't wait too long on this guy because he'll likely slip through the cracks and move to another residence. We must seal him inside that mansion before proceeding, which we'll discuss later."

"How can he move to another place? The other spirits I've connected with had attached to an object from personal ownership. Are you telling me Leonard can go wherever he wants?" That thought sent chills over my scalp and down my spine. "Grams?"

"Yes, I believe when you entered the mansion with your abilities, even with your smoky quartz crystal for protection – which it did protect you from him possessing you – he could piggyback you. In other words, he also has your abilities and can personally communicate with you like I'm doing right now, mind-talking, but I can only talk to you through Lucky. You can hear Leonard even when you can't see him. He's powerful."

"I don't understand. Piggyback me?" I didn't recall reading anything about that in Grams' journal. "It can't be because he has abilities similar to mine."

"You're right. Did you physically touch something in that house Leonard might have made or owned? Do you recall touching anything inside the house?"

I thought about when Kyle and I entered the mansion and how the negative energy had felt heavy and suffocating. "Kyle opened the front door as it was unlocked. Once inside, I ran past him, up the staircase, and down the hall to the last door. It's like something drew me, actually navigated me to stop at that room. I touched the arched, wooden door. Loud banging against it came from inside the room, messing with our hearing. Then I grabbed the ornate bronze cast doorknob. I noticed that because Gramps collected things like that doorknob. I wanted to open the door, but Kyle stopped me."

Lucky crawled closer to me. "Thank goodness Kyle was with you. I believe Leonard had manipulated you to open the door. His spirit might not be able to leave that room other than to mind-talk. Someone might have imprisoned him as he'd done to the women he controlled at that mansion."

"Grams, I saw him appear at the front door when we drove away, and also, when I had that blackout at Kyle's parents' house, Leonard and I stood at the front door of the mansion together." I thought about what might have taken place at that mansion. "Do you think there's an angry woman locked inside that room instead of Leonard? Or maybe more than one woman?"

"During those years, some women practiced 'black magic,' which is focused on dark energy, casting spells, using symbols, and specific ingredients. That can still happen today, but I've always practiced 'white magic,' using mantras, symbols, and specific ingredients focused on light energy. So, until we know what's inside that room, it could be either Leonard or one or more of the women."

Lucky jumped down, ran into the kitchen, and stopped at the door going into the garage.

I followed him. "You need to wait one minute for me. I need to get some clothes on." I turned around so fast that I ran into Kyle.

He grabbed me, so I didn't fall. "You're up early." He chuckled. "I'm dressed and can take Lucky outside. You better get dressed before I take advantage of the naked body under that robe."

I yanked the robe open, flashed my bare frontside at him, and then raced like the wind into the bedroom to dress.

48

"Not fair when the dog needs out!" Kyle hollered.

I quickly dressed, brushed my teeth and hair, and then hurried to the kitchen. Kyle walked in at the same time I entered.

"My turn to make breakfast." I pulled out a few utensils from the drawer.

"Take your time. It doesn't look like I'll be leaving anytime soon. We got dumped on again last night. I swear there's at least a foot or more of new snow. It's going to take forever for me to shovel the driveway." Kyle opened the door briefly and shook the snow from his coat, hat, and gloves.

"You just shook that snow into the garage." I stopped and stared at him.

"And you got dressed, leaving me high and dry." He stared right back, probably mirroring my stern face.

"Is this your first fight?" Grams asked. I looked at Lucky, who cocked his head while studying me.

"Grams just asked if this is our first fight." I smiled at Lucky and then at Kyle. "Do you think this is a fight, Kyle?"

"No. I'm checking Bri to see if I'll get some lovin' before breakfast." He chuckled as he took the rope leash off Lucky. "And the answer is?"

"No." I grabbed the egg carton, slice of ham, milk, and shredded cheese out of the fridge. "We've got work to do, making plans to evict Leonard from the earth realm."

"Whoa, who's Leonard?" Kyle's eyes studied me as he leaned against the counter.

"Grams told me the name of the evil entity inside the mansion. That's why she's here...to help us."

Kyle moved toward me. "That doesn't make me feel good about this spirit if your Grams' had to come back to help get him off the earth realm. What are we talking about? What can this thing actually do?"

"I have that same question. All I know is that the entity is powerful and has abilities, like getting inside my head and manipulating me. Grams understands it's going to take some extra special efforts, and that's why she's here."

"Sounds like we need to make a plan quickly, then. If that thing can hurt you, Bri, we need to eradicate it now." Kyle's face paled as he studied me. "I don't know how to save you from an evil spirit."

"We can strategize and devise a method to make it happen. Relax. We can't allow fear to overtake us," I said it out loud, sounding strong, but my insides churned like a blender mixing pudding.

"I understand that, but not having the ability to see this thing restricts me. Like fighting an invisible enemy in a horror story. There's no way to save the princess." Kyle's arms wrapped around me, pulling me close. Lucky ran over to us, whining and jumping on our legs. Kyle bent down and lifted him up as the puppy licked his fingers. "Okay,

Grams." Kyle made eye contact with Lucky. "I'm all in. What do we have to do to obliterate this thing?"

"Bri, tell him there's a way, and we'll figure it out. I wouldn't be here if there wasn't one."

I told Kyle what Grams told me, and then said, "That makes me feel better, knowing Grams is here because there is a way to beat this thing."

"Yea, that makes me feel better, too, knowing we're not on our own. We have knowledge and wisdom on our side." Kyle patted the puppy's head. "Thanks, Grams."

I leaned in and kissed Kyle's cheek. "Maybe we can meet over the internet on zoom or another program that allows us to discuss this with our team, and James, Sandy, and maybe Jacob also." I stepped over to a cupboard and pulled out a skillet, set it on the burner, and then dropped a splotch of butter into it. "I'll text Luke if you can text everyone else, Kyle."

"I can contact everyone, including Luke. You need to pull together all the info that Luke sent you and any info your Grams gives you. Then you can share it with the group by running the meeting. Give me a time, and I'll make sure everyone can make it."

"How about four-thirty this afternoon? Luke and Max get out of their classes by then and don't go into the restaurant tonight. They have Wednesdays off work."

"Okay, that's our game plan for after we've eaten. While you're cooking, I'm going to run to our neighbors, the Deans. They have a young dog about the size of Lucky. Maybe they'll share some of its food until we get to the store."

"Sounds perfect." I beat the eggs, quickly cut up the ham slice, added a bit of milk, and dumped it all into the warm pan.

Kyle rubbed a towel over Lucky, then filled a bowl with water and set it on the laundry room floor. Lucky gave him a gentle 'woof,' wiggling his rear end as if responding to Kyle's thoughtfulness.

"I'll be right back, Bri." Kyle headed out.

"You better hurry. Breakfast is almost ready," I hollered as the door slammed shut.

"Bri, your Kyle sort of reminds me of your grandfather." Grams' gentle mind-talk made me smile.

Chapter Five
Bri

After breakfast, I quickly bathed Lucky, making him look and smell like a new pup. Kyle had a food dish ready for him in the laundry room. While Lucky ate, Kyle and I headed to the sunroom.

We sat at the desk, reviewing all the newspaper articles and photographs from the library that Luke had sent me yesterday. A picture of the mansion from 1897, twelve years after being built, gave me goosebumps as I studied all the beautiful women and men dressed in the finest clothing of that time. They'd lined up in front, posing in male/female couples, toasting with flutes of most likely alcohol, several others struck a pose using different dance moves, or in a rapturous kiss appearing lustful. I counted ten couples, six extra women stood provocatively on the front steps, and two more posed in sensual undergarments at the arched doorway.

"Look at the women's faces." I moved so Kyle could study them.

"They certainly don't look as happy as their men folk, but it isn't easy to see with such fuzzy clarity."

"Yea, photos weren't the best back then. But those women look either scared or hopelessly miserable, which tells me they are probably captives." My sensitivities heightened in agreement. Those ladies didn't reside there because they liked it. "They hate it there."

"Look at this one." Kyle had moved to the next photo.

"That must be Dr. Leonard Whitenmeyer. He's a stunningly handsome man." He appeared so refined. I had a tough time thinking he could become evil. "What happened to him? What trauma turned him into a monster?"

"His father." Grams' voice slid through my brain. "He was also a doctor who never came home, oftentimes, not even during the night." Lucky sat at my feet, looking upward with his cute fluffy head cocked sideways.

I told Kyle what Grams had said. "Do you know why Leonard's father never came home? Was there something wrong with his mother? Or was his father a player?" I asked.

"I don't know much more than Leonard's father didn't have much to do with the home front, but he did take Leonard to work with him, allowing his child to witness surgeries. It's why Leonard became a doctor."

"He took a child into surgeries? That tells me Leonard's father had no filters for loving a child or the child's mother. Did the mother die? Why would he take his son into surgery?"

Kyle stared at me. "Your grams just told you Leonard's father took him as a child into surgeries? What the hell? That's traumatic for a kid." Kyle glanced at me and then down at Lucky. "What happened to Leonard's mother?"

"She came up missing. That's all I know. Maybe you can find out the 'why' another way," Grams said. Lucky jumped up, touching my thighs with his front paws.

I reached down, picked up the puppy, and sat him on my lap so he could look at the picture on my laptop screen.

"He certainly started as an enticingly handsome man," Grams said.

"And then turned into a Dr. Whitenmeyer – Mr. Hide," I added. Then I repeated what Grams said to Kyle, which led to my comment. There wasn't much else we found in the news, nothing more about the house. "One of the women I saw, a couple of miles down the road from the mansion, told me to 'stay away.' If I return to that area, I wonder if I can ask her some questions."

"Bri, I insist on going with you every time any of you visit there. Would you place a smoky quartz crystal on Lucky to protect us?" Lucky turned on my lap to stare at me.

I gave him a giant hug. "Of course." I looked at Kyle. "We need a collar and a leash for Lucky. Grams insists on going with anyone that visits the mansion and wants me to put a smoky quartz crystal on the pup for protection."

Kyle rubbed the back of Lucky's head. "Grams, you know we'll do everything you ask. And I'm so glad you're here with us. Especially for this case, so Bri stays safe." Lucky drew his paws from my lap and placed them on Kyle's.

"I trust your Kyle," Grams said. "He so reminds me of Fred." Then Lucky licked Kyle's hand.

"Lucky and Grams, thanks for being here." Kyle patted the dog's head again and slid the pup back on my lap. He stood and pushed his chair against the wall.

"Grams says you remind her of my gramps." I glanced out the window at the continuing snow.

"I like your gramps." He patted Lucky's head again. "And your grams."

"When will we be able to get out to that mansion? It's crazy weather." I closed my laptop. "I'll help you shovel the driveway, so maybe we can get into town. I'm getting stir-crazy."

"Okay. If we can get into town, maybe we can go farther and meet up with Max and Luke. Have the Zoom meeting with Sandy, James, and your ghost guardian team." He chuckled and grabbed me, pulling me close. "I want you to listen to your grams, though. Please be careful with this case. I felt fear for you at Dad's house, Bri. Like a horror movie, your eyes rolled back when you blanked out."

"Well, it was a horror movie. Leonard Whitenmeyer terrified me."

* * *

"Wow, babe, you were like a little snowblower with all that shoveling you did." Kyle grabbed my hand for a short squeeze as we pulled out of our driveway. Lucky sat in the back with my laptop case. His dog dishes, food, water bottle, and a suitcase of extra clothes got loaded in the back of the SUV should we end up staying in the hotel. Kyle also packed a snow shovel, a scraper, a box with two blankets, a candle, a lighter, and a flashlight.

"And you pack like a boy scout." I sat up straighter to see if I could make out the edges of the road. "There are no tire tracks."

"This vehicle has snow tires and four-wheel drive. We'll be all right." He stopped at the sign. No traffic, but some vehicles had driven over the main street into town. We passed the road to our parents' homes and saw tire tracks. "I bet Dad drove into work this morning."

Kyle went slow, passing a couple of empty cars that had slid into the ditch.

"I think we should head toward Kalamazoo. I'll text Luke to make sure they're at the hotel and are staying another night there."

"Yea, we could get a room where they're staying if they allow dogs." He hit a drift, and the SUV slid over to the edge but straightened just in the nick of time. "Dang, that was a close one."

So, then I concentrated on texting Luke: *'Hey, would you and Max be up for company at your hotel, provided the place allows dogs? We got one and can't wait for you to meet him. We need to have a Zoom meeting together with James and Sandy. We thought we'd spend the night at the hotel if you and Max are planning to stay another night.'*

"Wow, the wind picked up just since we've been on the road. Look at that white-out." Kyle cranked up the windshield wipers and slowed the SUV even more. "I hope everyone is driving with their lights on." Just then, two flashing tail lights appeared. Kyle pulled off to the right and then stopped behind the truck. "It's Dad. You stay here with Lucky." Kyle shut the door and ran to the driver's side of his dad's vehicle.

"Grams, you here?" I turned toward Lucky, who, of course, thought I spoke to him. "Who's a good boy?" I brushed my hand over the top of the pup's head as his tongue lapped my coat sleeve. Grams didn't respond, which concerned me. I needed to ask her questions about where she goes when she's not inside Lucky and how she got here in the first place. Who directs her? It seemed like the case took over my entire brain. I hadn't even mentioned Grams to my gramps.

Finally, Kyle walked back to the SUV and jumped inside. "Dad had stopped to help the car ahead of him. They were in the ditch, so I helped also, and we got their car back on the road."

"So, are we following your dad to the police station?" If we did, I knew Kyle would want to stay.

"I'm going to drive that way, not to the station, but to take that street toward Luke and Max's hotel. There's a huge string of accidents on the highway going toward Kalamazoo. Dad said the Portage and Kalamazoo main streets got plowed early this morning."

"I haven't heard back from Luke yet, unlike him if he isn't in class today. Maybe they did have class after all."

"Hey, let's swing into the pet store to grab a couple of toys and some food for Lucky." Kyle turned into their parking lot before I could answer.

"We can't take him in without a leash, so maybe I should go in and grab the stuff. You stay with Lucky. Grams isn't here at the moment." I didn't give Kyle time to respond and hurried inside the store. I purchased the necessary stuff and headed back to the SUV, which got moved. I looked around the parking lot, then noticed the vehicle coming toward me.

Kyle waved me inside.

"Where'd you go?" I climbed inside, dropped the bags at my feet, and hauled a toy out for Lucky. He gently pulled it out of my hand. "Good, boy."

"Somebody had to potty, so I drove us to the edge of the parking lot. Thank goodness I brought the rope I used for his leash. So, what did you get for him." Kyle pulled out of the parking lot and onto the street. "Even though the roads got plowed here, there's not a lot of traffic."

I flashed the stuff I bought at Kyle and then at Lucky, who seemed to know everything belonged to him after sniffing it. My phone indicated a call. I answered, "Hey, I thought maybe you'd flown to the moon or something." I set it on speaker.

"We didn't have class today, so Max and I went to the hotel restaurant for a late breakfast or early lunch, and both of us left our phones in the room. I just now saw your text." Luke sounded so happy after all the trauma he'd gone through in his younger years. Max fixed all the broken parts inside Luke, and I adored hearing my best friend's joy-filled voice.

"Well, we're on our way to your hotel now. In fact, we're not too far from there. Do you know if they allow dogs? And can we do the Zoom meeting there with all of us?"

"I know they allow dogs because we saw a woman walking out the door with one earlier. We planned on hanging out here today, so we can have the Zoom meeting in our room. It's giant-sized." Luke told Max our plan, and I heard him agree to it.

"Okay, hopefully, they'll have a room for us, and we'll see you soon." After I hung up, Luke texted me their room number.

"Good show, kiddo. It looks like we're having a mini vacation with the boys and our trusty dog." Kyle grinned as he pulled into the parking ramp of the hotel. "Let's eat before we go find Max and Luke. After all the driveway shoveling and pushing a car out of a drift, I'm famished."

"Me, too."

* * *

After we checked in and ate, Kyle took Lucky out to potty while I cleared away the meal stuff and grabbed my laptop. I'd just sat on the edge of the bed when I experienced a whole-body chill. My hands trembled as I stared at them. Then my lights must have gone out because I found myself in front of the mansion. Leonard stood at the doorway. What was once a handsome man had turned into a wild-eyed, pointed-toothed, long-nailed freak of nature.

"How yummy of you to visit me on such short notice." His tongue slathered across his lips like a hungry, crazed monster.

I stepped back, wanting to run in the opposite direction, but my body turned into a paralyzed statue. My mouth wouldn't open, even though my eyes seemed glued open, unblinking.

"I wouldn't want you to miss a thing that I'm going to do to you." His forefinger nail slid down my face and across my lips. He lifted his head and laughed, a horrible sound that made everything inside me want to scream. "You, my dear, will become a great playmate."

Suddenly, a dog barked somewhere behind me. Hope rose until the monster-man pulled me into a squeezing hold, and his long, slobbery tongue entered my ear. "I'm going to make you mine," he whispered.

* * *

Kyle

I opened our hotel room door, and Lucky went flying inside. He jumped on the bed, barking his head off at Bri's prone body.

"Bri, wake up!" Her pale face was nothing compared to her ice-cold body. I shook her and then rubbed my hands over her arms. "Bri," I repeated over and over into her ears.

Lucky kept licking her face or barking in her ear as if directed.

"Grams, if you're inside Lucky, please do something. It feels like Bri's not going to come around." I couldn't hear Grams, nor any spirit, let alone see them. I pulled Bri's clothes off, picked her up, setting her inside the shower, and turned on the cold water. She lay there, oblivious to anything around her, not feeling the water or hearing my voice. I turned off the water and covered her with a towel. Then I called James.

"Do you guys want to meet earlier?" James' first question, not knowing why I called.

I explained how I'd found Bri while studying her unmoving body in the bathtub. And then I told him what happened with her at Dad's. She hadn't awakened like last time. "Do you know of anything I can do to awaken her?"

"Well, putting her in the tub and running cold water over her should have brought her around. Let me talk to Sandy, and I'll call you right back."

Lucky jumped out of the tub and ran toward the bed. I followed him. He went straight to the bedstand and grabbed Bri's necklace with his teeth. He turned to me with the thing dangling from his mouth and shot across the bed back to me.

I stared at the necklace. "Oh, my Gods, this is her protection." I ran into the bathroom and sat her up to slip the cord over her head. "Come on, Bri. Come back to me." I gently shook her, then leaned in and kissed her. "Bri, I need you. Come back." I repeated those words three times like she'd taught us to do with mantras.

Lucky barked, jumping into the tub and onto her legs. Almost as if the dog screamed at her, he kept barking in her face.

I finally had to pull him off her. "You're going to get us bounced out of here if you don't quiet down." Then I looked at Bri. Her eyes, filled with panic, stared back at me as her hand clasped the smoky quartz crystal.

Chapter Six

Bri

I worked hard to gain my bearing as I glanced around the room. My parched mouth took a moment to salivate. "Some water, please," I rasped.

"Bri, why'd you take off your smoky quartz crystal?" Grams asked. Lucky stood over me, staring.

"To protect you and Lucky," I croaked, and it seemed the extent of my words.

Kyle plopped beside me on the bed and held the glass of water to my lips. "Drink up, buttercup."

I choked a little, and some dribbled out of my mouth, but I continued slurping all of it.

"Can you tell us what happened? You were out of it for at least a half hour, if not longer. Where'd you go?" Kyle set the cup on the bedstand.

"I didn't have my smoky quartz necklace on because I intended to use it for Lucky's collar we'd just purchased." I stopped and strained to swallow. "More water, please."

"Dear, I'm attempting to read your mind, but there's a blockage. Do you remember anything?" Grams' voice resonated through my head, yet Lucky's wet paw settled on my trembling hand as if he were the one communicating with me.

I remembered everything and feared no one would believe what that spirit could do. I certainly didn't want my grandmother to witness any of the terrifying crap that spectral inflicted on me.

Kyle reached across with the glass of water and touched my lips, and I emptied it again.

My throat responded this time, feeling soothed. "I counted a lot of hours, not minutes." I heard the quiver in my voice. "Evil Leonard abused me in ways I don't wish to share." I raised my arms and looked them over, expecting to find cuts, burns, and bleeding from the ropes around my wrists and ankles. I saw nothing from all his torturous, pain-inflicting attempts to get me to promise that I would stay with him. He would use the people closest to me as his targets if I didn't. So, what would happen?

"You're naked, my sweet. I tried a cold-water shower to wake you. It didn't work. Neither did Lucky's barking in your face."

"His bark was the last thing I heard from here, then Leonard took over, paralyzing me. I couldn't talk or scream. So much pain. hours and hours of it. How did any of those women survive for any length of time?" Tears rolled down my cheeks, and I quickly wiped them away. I would not fall prey to his malicious actions.

A knock on the door drew Kyle away. When he opened it, I heard Luke and Max's voices. I quickly slid under the blankets.

"Why are you in bed, dear heart?" Luke grinned as his brows went up and down. "No, maybe it's best not to tell me any details." They all chuckled.

"Hey, listen," Kyle whispered, pulling the guys back into the alcove near the entry, "she's been through something horrifying. She's just now coming around from it. I couldn't wake her. We think the same ghost that knocked her out at Dad's the other night came back and captured her spirit again. She finally opened her eyes when I put her smoky quartz necklace over her head. She said she's been gone for hours, lots of them, not minutes, and that monster tortured her."

I heard every whispered word as if I stood right next to Kyle. Lucky stood over me, staring. "Grams, I hear Kyle's whispered words as if he's standing beside me. What's happened to me?"

"I believe that monster can hear through you, also. We're dealing with something I only heard about but never dealt with myself. Hum right now and grab a pencil and paper."

I hummed and pulled a pen and paper out of the bed stand. Lucky chimed in with a puppy whine.

Grams whispered, and I wrote. "You'll need to research, and then we must do some testing to get it right."

I'd written what she said, wondering if the spirit could hear Gram's voice inside my head, even with my humming. Then I showed Lucky the paper. He nodded and blinked in acknowledgment. The guys stepped into the room from the alcove, attentive to Lucky and the note in my hand.

"What's with all the humming?" Max asked.

Before I could answer, Luke jumped on the bed. "Who's a good boy?" He roughed the fur around Lucky's head, then slid the pup toward him for a big hug. "Hello, Lucky."

"Hey." I waited for all heads to turn and then lifted the note. After they had a moment to read, I quickly wrote more, 'Grams and I believe the spirit amped my hearing because it's also listening. We need to be careful what anyone says around me.' All the guys nodded.

Then Kyle asked, "How about we head downstairs to the bar for a quick one while Bri gets dressed?" He looked at Lucky, who nodded and blinked. Grams must have it down with the pup for the acknowledgment gestures.

The pup made me smile. I grabbed Lucky's collar because he wanted to go with the guys after Luke's hug. "You get to stay with me, cutie. I think you're an angel."

Grams said, "I believe you're correct."

***

Kyle

When we entered the bar, I chose a table in a corner away from everyone.

"So, what did you mean that Bri got tortured?" Luke's jaw tightened as he stared. "Whatever we're messing with has power, I mean a lot of it. Bri's never gotten taken over like that, and she's dealt with some real hard-ass spirits."

"The way she came back into her body as soon as I placed her smoky quartz crystal necklace back over her head tells me that we all need to carry protection. Make sure you have one if not two of those crystals on your person – in a pocket or around your neck. We can't afford to lose anyone to whatever that thing is." All I kept thinking about was the look on Bri's face when she awakened. "When her eyes opened, they were full of panic, her hands trembled, and her whole body shook. She mentioned getting paralyzed and then painfully tortured for hours when she'd only been out for maybe thirty minutes."

"Well, she's the only one that can hear her grams, who happens to be the only one with all the suggestions of getting rid of the spirit. Talk about a challenge. I mean, it's not like the dog can write Grams' communications. We're in the dark on this."

Luke sighed, shaking his head. "I don't like it. Did you notice how pale Bri looked?"

"Of course, I noticed. I've never felt such fear as when I couldn't get Bri to wake up." And I continued having that feeling every second, which reminded me to ask Bri how long her grams can stay whenever she visits.

Right then, a waitress stepped over to the table. "You boys looking for drinks or food or both?"

"I could do both," Luke said. "Should we order something for Bri also?"

We all ordered a beer, and the waitress left menus and silverware on the table as she rushed off to get our beers.

Right then, I caught movement at the opened bar doorway. "Bri. Be right back." I hurried over to her.

"I left Lucky in the room with a toy. Not sure how good he'll be without us, so I'm not staying."

I pulled her to my side, and we walked to the table. I grabbed a menu. "Check it over. I know we ate not long ago, but you might be starving after what you've been through."

Bri shook her head. "Nope, not hungry, but maybe a soda to settle my stomach?"

"We're going to finish our beers and head back to the room, but I'll take you back with a soda to go right now, then come back down." I glanced toward the guys. "I'll be back."

"You stay up there with Bri. We'll bring some beers and our food to your room. We can hang out with you two for a while, but maybe we should do the Zoom in our room without you, Bri. I can take notes for Kyle." Luke winked at Bri, not giving anything away that might alert the evil spirit.

"Thanks, guys. See you in a little while." I wrapped an arm around Bri's waist and walked to the elevator. "I'm glad you're feeling better, even though you're still pale as a ghost. You had me a wreck, woman."

"I'm not sure I'm up to company tonight, Kyle. I didn't want to say it in front of Luke and Max. Not sure how I'm going to sleep as I'm honestly afraid to close my eyes for longer than a blink."

I felt her shiver and squeezed her tighter to my side. When we got to our room, I opened the door, and Lucky sat in the alcove, waiting for us. That dog opened my heart when he went crazy to wake up Bri. He would make an excellent protector.

"Hi, Lucky." The pup wagged his tail as if it were on fire as he ran to Bri. She huddled down on her knees and hugged him. He pushed the side of his head into her. "I love you, little man."

"It's undeniable that he loves you too." Watching them together made me happy that I brought him home.

"Kyle, I can attend the Zoom meeting from here." She ran to her notes and wrote, 'I can have it on mute so I won't feel alone, and then you can see me too.'

"Good idea. I'll text Luke and let him know to invite you. We're inviting the new guy also. See if he can get here. If not, we can text him an invite to the Zoom." I grabbed her paper and wrote, 'Jacob.'

"Good thinking." Her brows rose, and she nodded. "You're quite the detective, Mr. Benton."

"You're quite the specialist, Ms. Lancaster." Then I added another note, 'I'm sorry you had to suffer so much pain. Do you know what that monster hoped to gain by torturing you?'

* * *

Bri

I didn't want to tell Kyle about the promise – Leonard would only stop if I promised to stay with him. My friends could get blindsided if I didn't stay with the evil spirit. He would use them as his targets if I left him, and I had. How could that crazy, malicious spirit figure out who they were, and how could he enter their minds? What would he do to someone unable to see or hear him? I grabbed the paper away from Kyle and wrote my thoughts and the promise that the madman spirit expected of me. When I handed it back to Kyle, his breath caught. I raised a finger and shook my head so he wouldn't say anything.

"I will find a way to communicate with you, even through this." He waved the paper and pen in the air. "We will figure this out. I'll let you know about it afterward." He raised a brow to remind me of the upcoming meeting without saying it out loud.

Kyle left the room, and about forty-five minutes later, the invitation to the internet meeting came through my laptop. I signed on and then hit mute. I saw Jacob for the first time. He appeared close to our age or a few years older, with reddish hair, a groomed stash and beard, and the greenest eyes I'd ever seen, like Mom's. James and Sandy came on together, and so had Kyle, Luke, and Max. Everyone waved at each other, then joked around for a moment.

Lucky lay beside me on the bed as I sat with my laptop. It didn't take long for the meeting to get serious. I attempted to lip-read and got some words, but I usually missed most of the sentences. It seemed like the meeting lasted forever, and I hadn't heard from Grams since Kyle and I returned from the bar. Kyle must have explained what had happened to me with James, Sandy, and Jacob because no one addressed me, and I said nothing in return.

Until I knew the spirit didn't hijack my hearing any longer, I couldn't ask Grams any of the questions I wanted to ask her. I sipped the soda whenever my eyes got heavy-lidded. I should have ordered a cola, not one without caffeine. I set my computer on the bed and looked for something to read. Nothing. I turned on the television, looking for a comedy. Everything seemed tagged as either a thriller or a horror theme.

I returned to my laptop, but the Zoom had ended without me. Then the entrance door opened, and Lucky sprang off the bed, rushing into the alcove.

"There's a good boy," Kyle's voice brought tears to my eyes. He walked over to me. "We have our first plan of action and several other possibilities. I'm hopeful, Bri." He handed me several small notebooks and a couple of pens. His smile dazzled, like always. "We all want you to stay in communication, so we decided to load you up with a few supplies. You can thank Luke for most of the contributions. I think he emptied his chef training bag of note-taking gear, dedicating them to his soul-mate bestie."

That planted a big ole smile on my face. "When do we get started?" I stacked the notebooks and set the pens aside.

Kyle grabbed a notebook and pen and started writing like a madman. He sat on the edge of the bed, still writing. 'We plan on bringing a lot of gear to the mansion tomorrow night or the following night, depending on the road conditions. I'm hoping your grams can give you information on what to expect, a solid ceremony to extricate the beast, or at least, how all of us can stay protected while we do our best to remove this crazed lunatic from the earth plane or realm, or however you say it.'

I read as he wrote, and when he finished, I grabbed another notebook and pen. 'I'm not sure how to communicate best with Grams as I'm the only one that can hear her, and that heinous entity is listening. It's not like Grams can write notes to us using Lucky's paws. Maybe I can write notes to her, and she can either nod or shake her head through Lucky.'

"I know that will take much longer, Bri," he said aloud. His expression softened as those striking blues stole my breath. "But I think that's the only good way, considering there are no other options." Kyle stood and pulled me close. His warmth penetrated my body as his arms tightened around me. "I can't lose you again." His strong heartbeat reverberated through my chest, and his heated breath against my hair sent tingles down my spine, like a zipline snapping along my nerve endings.

I closed my eyes, feeling safe, secure, and protected, until an ominous voice darted through my brain, "He has already lost you." A menacing laugh cackled inside my head, and he obnoxiously added, "I have marked you. You are mine."

Chapter Seven

Bri

Kyle and I watched a comedy detective movie in bed until he fell asleep with Lucky, who wiped out at the foot of the bed, honking little puppy snores. I got up, made a cup of coffee to stay awake, and then took the elevator to the lobby to find mile to add to my cup and something stimulating for wakefulness. Dad's hotels had several different shops, bars, and smaller restaurants for those who didn't want to eat at the NL Cuisine Royale attached to the Northern Lights Royale Hotel, where we spent the night. I walked by the open double door of the first bar restaurant called, Star Gazer Bar & Grill, and peeked inside. Luke and Max were the only customers, so I headed toward their table.

"Hi, friends."

They looked up simultaneously, but Luke smiled much more extensively than Max. "What's up, buttercup? Wanna cocktail?" Luke grinned.

"No, I'm actually trying not to close my eyes. Seems bad things happen when my lights go out."

Max jumped up and pulled out a chair, motioning for me to sit. "Ma Lady."

"Thanks, Max." I was impressed. Unlike the many times we didn't hit it off so well, Max and I had become good friends. Luke and Max made a complex but wonderful couple. Luke found his mate and a whole new world changed him into a happy, positive person. Max had a similar outcome to Luke.

"So..., we know there are limitations on subject matter for conversations, but I want to know how you're feeling? Safe, confused, terrified, happy, etc.?" Luke studied my face after each word.

"All of the above," I stated. "But with determination and confidence for success. Does that make sense?"

"Absolutely." Max lifted his beer bottle as if for a toast. "You are our fearless leader, after all."

And I knew what he meant. They would follow my lead and do whatever it took to make the evil spirit disappear from the earth realm. I relaxed against the chair, feeling comfort and companionship with Luke and Max.

"Where's Kyle?" Luke shook his empty bottle toward the waitress. She nodded and raised her finger. Then Max lifted his, and she raised two fingers.

"Be right there," she stated.

"Kyle and Lucky fell asleep, and I don't want to close my eyes, so here I am."

"Hey, Kerry, bring a cherry coke in a glass of ice also, please," Luke said as he turned toward the bar, where the waitress grabbed their beers from the refrigerator.

"Gotcha covered."

"So, you boys know the waitress's name. You are rated 'excellent customers,' I'm sure." I nodded and grinned.

The guys smiled as Kerry hurried back with the goods on a tray. She even left a dish of nuts in the middle of the table. "Just holler if you want anything else. I'll keep the place open for a few more hours tonight."

Max handed her some money. "Keep the change, Kerry."

"Max and I have gotten to know Kerry because we are interning at your dad's NL Cuisine restaurant. We stop in this bar occasionally, and she works a lot of hours, so we've become sorta friends." Luke shuffled up from his chair. "Hey, if you want to stay awake for a while, how about a game of darts? It's been a while since we've played that. Maybe I can win a game or two."

"I call the greens." I knew that would knock Luke down a peg, as that was his favorite dart color.

"You little minx. Now, I'm for sure going to win. My favorites changed to reds months ago." He chuckled, making me realize he had lied.

We played darts for a couple of hours, and then Kerry stopped by our table and said, "Time to call it a night, everyone."

Luke quickly put the darts away next to the dart board. And Max grabbed a tray off the bar, placing all the stuff from our table on it. I carried it back to the bar and thanked Kerry again for staying open. The guys strode over and left Kerry a nice tip.

We left and walked to the elevator. Luke tapped the third-floor button.

"Tell me that both of you have a smoky quartz crystal on you for protection. And that you'll be wearing it, even in your sleep."

Max and Luke lifted their leather strapped necklaces from inside their shirts to dangle the smoky crystal in front of my face.

"Bravo, boys." I clapped for effect. "Please, wear it always, especially right now. There are threats." I raised my brows and tilted my head to enhance the warning.

They nodded and slipped the gemstones inside their shirts. The guys walked me to my room and waited for me to open the door.

"Bri, if you need us, just call. You know I'm a light sleeper," Luke said.

"Thanks, both of you. I'll be fine. We'll have things righted soon." As the words popped out of my mouth, I hoped to heck the nut-ball spirit wasn't putting anything together. I worked all the words through my brain before saying anything out loud, conscientious of the listener that could likely damage any action plan if he overheard any clues. I waved goodbye to Luke and Max, then closed the door and bolted it. *Now,*

79

what do I do to stay awake? I didn't think to bring my electronic book.

I stood in the foyer and listened to ensure Kyle and Lucky were still asleep. A little rustle made me peek around the corner, and Lucky stood on the bed with his head cocked to the side, staring at me. His cute, furry legs pranced, and he gave an excited yip.

"Shhh, Lucky, come," I whispered loud enough for the pup to hear me.

Kyle's eyes were still closed as he patted the bed for the dog. Then his hand extended to my side, and his eyes opened wide. He sat up, looking wildly around the room, and then I stepped farther inside so he could see me.

"I'm sorry that I woke you." I went to his side of the bed and sat on the edge.

"Why didn't you wake me? Is everything okay?" He grasped my hand and pulled me closer.

"Honestly, I'm afraid to fall asleep. I can't say much, knowing we likely have a listener."

"I should have guessed that, and why I didn't think about it is beyond me." Now Kyle appeared wide awake. "Shall we watch a movie?" He glanced at the bedside clock. "You've been up for hours, Bri. How will you function..."

"We've already watched a movie." I quickly raised my finger to his lips and mouthed: "Not out loud."

Lucky snuggled between Kyle's body and mine.

"Grams?" I stared at the puppy, waiting for any communication. "I hope all is well." I glanced at Kyle. "This is a first for her; she might not know any of the limitations."

Kyle patted the pup. "You don't suppose something similar to what happened to you has happened to your grams, do you?" He clicked on the lamp from the nightstand buttons.

I nodded toward my pile of notebooks and a stash of pens and grabbed one of each. Kyle watched as I wrote. 'I don't think Grams would get the same treatment as I did. I think Grams' torture might become even more painful.' I thought about the possibilities of what Leonard might do with Grams being a spirit brought back to the earth realm. The curtains had remained open, and the outside lighting made it easy to see the accumulating snow. I slid off the bed and walked to the window, looking down at the lumps of white in the parking lot...snow covered the vehicles. The road beyond hadn't gotten plowed, but tire tracks had kept it usable.

Kyle stepped over, pressing his body into my backside, and wrapping his arms around me.

My breath caught, and I gasped, "You're completely naked." I attempted to turn around, but he kept me in our sensual position, his warm breath and lips brushing my neck.

"I know an excellent way for you to stay awake," he whispered as his hands slid under my shirt and cupped my breasts.

Other regions of his body came alive, as did mine.

Lucky yipped and jumped off the bed, rushing over to bark at us.

"Okay, little fella, you're sleeping inside the box tonight." Kyle led me toward the bed with Lucky yipping all the way.

"But we didn't bring his box inside. You used it to pack the car safety stuff."

"He's getting a drawer with a blanket and will love it." Kyle slipped on his underwear and pulled a drawer out of the dresser.

I dashed into the bathroom to shower. The warm water from the showerhead dropped like a gentle rain over my body, building inner and outer sensitivities in preparation for what might come next. Quickly, I soaped up, cleansing and rinsing. I enjoyed our intimacy lately and hoped that part of our relationship would never grow old.

The bathroom door opened and closed, and a few seconds later, Kyle slipped into the shower. He stepped behind me, and his arms wrapped around my waist, pulling my backside into him. "I love you, Bri," he whispered, tenderly kissing my ear. The rest of our exploring touches to each other flowed slowly and naturally, eventually leaving us panting on the floor with the warm water drops cleansing every inch of us. I felt so sated and sleepy, wanting to climb into that bed and snuggle against Kyle.

My traumatic horror experience with the terrifying Mr. Whitenmeyer whipped vividly inside my brain, sending lightning strikes throughout my body. Time to get dressed before I fell asleep, and that monster continued his terrorizing and painful experiments on every part of my body.

* * *

Kyle

I'd already dressed when Bri walked out of the bathroom. Her natural beauty always warmed me, like her ever-caring personality. She glanced my way and blushed, slipping on her undergarments, and then finishing with jeans and a sweatshirt. I'd gotten about four hours of sleep and figured I could keep up with her determination to research, even though the clock showed three-thirty a.m.

Bri climbed onto the bed and settled against the headboard, with notes beside her and the computer opened. The pup remained asleep in the drawer I'd set beside the bed. The scene of Bri and the puppy reminded me of a Christmas Card with the bed next to the window, showing the falling snow that glistened from the parking lot lights.

She looked up at me and patted the bed. "Come sit beside me so you can see what I'm seeing, and we don't have to talk about it."

Lucky heard her voice and climbed out of the drawer. He attempted to jump on the bed, but it was too high for the little guy.

"Okay, you can join us." I picked him up and set him next to Bri. He circled beside her until he finally snuggled into her thigh and laid down.

Bri gave him a little pat on the head and smoothed the fur down his back. "I love this little guy."

"So do I. Lucky gets us. He already knows us, and I think we know him too. And not because sometimes your grandmother resides in him." I walked around the bed to sit on the other side of Bri. "Let's get to it."

Her fingers clicked across the keys, bringing up all kinds of pictures she'd downloaded onto her laptop from Luke's texts. Then a picture of Leonard Whitenmeyer appeared, and her breath sucked in. "What happened to this man?" She shook her head. "He looks nothing like that now. Long sharp nails, pointed teeth, a long slithering tongue, and his eyes are so dark, wild, and demanding. It's as if he can look right through me and see my soul."

Then my breath caught. "Maybe you need to keep certain things on paper." I raised my brows and handed her a notebook and pen.

Bri clicked through a few more pictures and stopped at the one where women had posed on the porch and in the doorway. She pointed at two of the women, nodding her head, and then grabbed her notebook and pen and wrote, 'These were the two women I saw on our way home. The woman I saw in the third-story window isn't in any of these pictures.' She ran through several more pictures, stopped at one, and wrote, 'There she is.'

I studied the picture. Bri enlarged it, but that didn't make it clearer. The woman appeared young, like a teenager. All the women in those pictures looked young with over-endowed breasts. I wrote, 'Do you think that monster surgically changed their bodies?'

Bri studied the pictures as she moved through them again. "Yes." She jotted another note, 'He made them all little Frankensteinettes with enormous breasts. I wonder what else he changed on them.'

I wrote, 'Can you imagine the pain they went through? That happened way before plastic surgery got introduced to the medical world. How many women do you think suffered at his hand?' I couldn't wrap my head around it. Those young women, more likely teen girls, had gone through terrorizing hell and were surely left with scars and pain. I wrote more, 'Whitenmeyer was a monster of the worst kind, a pedophile with a surgical knife.'

Chapter Eight

Bri

"I could use another cup of coffee. How about you?" I slid off the bed while Kyle placed the leash on Lucky. The nightstand clock read 6:00 a.m. I needed to do something other than read more about Whitenmeyer or look at any posted pictures of his place. We had spent hours doing that. "Let me take Lucky outside to potty." Cold air would keep me alert.

"I'll go with you, and we can see if there's a place to walk. I heard some snowplowing earlier, so maybe we can drive to James and Sandy's and..." Kyle picked up a notebook and pen, dropping them on the colossal dresser where I would see them when we returned. He added, "And write out an action plan."

"Yea, that sounds good. I need fresh air and another cup of coffee to keep me awake. We ran out of cream, so I'll grab coffee and cream from the lobby coffee station."

Kyle slipped into his coat and boots, grabbed the end of Lucky's leash, and headed for the door. "Get me a coffee too."

I took my coat off the hanger, slipped into my boots, and followed him.

"You got everything you need?" he asked. Right then, someone tapped on the door. Kyle opened it.

"Hey, dudes," I said to Luke and Max.

"We're going downstairs for breakfast and wondered if you'd care to join us?" Luke asked. He bent down and picked up Lucky. "Who's a good boy," he said, repeating that as he playfully rubbed Lucky's back and ears.

"The dog needs to go out for a potty and then I'll take him back to the room. We want to sit with you for breakfast if you can wait a few minutes before you start eating." Kyle snatched Lucky from Luke. "Unless you make Lucky potty in the hallway."

Luke backed away with his hands raised in front of him as if Kyle pointed a gun at him. "Oh, geez, sorry about that. You probably should hurry."

"We'll wait for you at a table," Max said, slapping Luke on the back. "Come on, funny man. No more puppy play."

We followed them into the elevator, and when we got to the ground floor, they headed toward the Breakfast Niche restaurant, and we hurried toward the lobby's front door for Lucky's potty time.

"I'm getting the coffees, and then I'll be right out." I didn't wait for an answer as I turned toward the coffee station.

Kyle hollered, "I'll be around the right side of the building."

When I found them, I handed Kyle his cup. "Looks like the little guy did his numbers."

"You wouldn't happen to have a doggie bag on you, would you?" Kyle sipped the coffee. "Oh, that's strong."

I had tucked a roll of bags in my pocket from the box I'd gotten at the dog store. "Gotcha covered." I took Lucky's leash and handed Kyle my cup while I did the pick-up. The little guy just sat in the snow, waiting for me to finish. "I saw a dumpster off to the side of the entry. I'll run the bag over there. Here's the leash, and I'll take my coffee." We exchanged, and Kyle followed me with Lucky tucked against his side, one arm wrapped around him. The little guy had gotten shivering cold.

"I'll run Lucky to our room, and you go find the guys. I won't be more than a few minutes." Kyle headed toward the elevator.

I watched him walk across the lobby on a mission, all broad shoulders with his manly swagger. He waved at me with a giant smile as the elevator door closed, and I realized that I still stood in the center of the lobby. I chalked it up to falling asleep with my eyes open and mouth drooling.

As I entered the Breakfast Niche restaurant, Luke waved me over. I noticed hardly any patrons sitting inside. Most that walked in collected to-go bags at the front. I was sure the weather had something to do with that. Airports in and around the area had shut down due to the heavy snow conditions. The carry-out peeps probably went to work in their hotel room. I walked over to the booth in the far corner where Luke and Max were chuckling about something Max had just said.

"Good morning, Sunshine." Luke gave me a hand salute. "So, Kyle took the task of dropping off Lucky at the room. Well trained, Bri."

I stared at him. "Don't give me any guff today, Luke."

He immediately startled backward, eyes wide, then spread two fingers in the peace symbol.

Yea, I deserved that. "You know I haven't gotten a lot of sleep, and when I don't, I get emotional, which can go either way. I cry, or I get mad. Do you honestly want to mess around with that roller-coaster ride?"

Max laughed, and when I turned toward him, he laughed harder, reminding me of the ass-act he used to give me years ago when we were in high school.

"Wasn't that funny, Max." I took a deep breath and a big swallow of the coffee I had carried in. "Okay, so what did you order?"

Kyle walked in and hurried over to our booth. "You haven't started eating yet?" He slid into the seat and picked up a menu. "Has anyone ordered?"

"Not yet. We got today off from class, and due to the low possibility of people coming into NL Cuisine Restaurant," Max glanced at me, "your dad gave us another day off from chef-dom." Max turned toward Kyle. "So, Luke called James to check on the road conditions out to his place. There's a good chance we can drive to SPI from here."

"Yea, a plow went by earlier this morning. I still wouldn't want to take the highway due to the crazy drivers who don't know how to drive at a slow speed in winter. I'm game to try if you guys are up to it." Kyle slid closer to Bri. "What do you think? Do you feel comfortable driving to SPI?"

I wanted to snuggle in bed with Kyle and fall asleep, but that wouldn't happen until we slew the dragon. "Yes, I think we need to come up with our plan." I glanced around the table. "We need to get the ball rolling." If Whitenmeyer listened in, he wouldn't understand my figure of speech and certainly wouldn't have a clue about SPI.

I picked up a menu and decided on baked oatmeal with chopped apples, walnuts, and maple syrup. The waitress came and took everyone's order as she filled coffee cups. I got my refill in the tall, insulated cup from the lobby but asked for a small glass of milk to use as a creamer.

Kyle texted James, telling him we would be there this morning.

The guy's got some good laughs while we ate, enough to keep my mind occupied and away from Whitenmeyer. Eventually, we went to our rooms to pack. Luke and Max didn't have any packing because they planned on spending another night at the hotel. They also decided to drive separately. I thought it might have something to do with conversations overheard by Whitenmeyer, but it's because they probably wouldn't want to put us out by running them back to the hotel when we finished at SPI.

When we entered our room, I went directly to Lucky. "Grams, are you here?" Kyle followed and waited beside me. The pup practically bounced out of the drawer and ran to us.

"Anything?" Kyle grabbed the leash.

I shook my head. "I'll pack if you want to run him back outside. Everything is still in the suitcase, and Lucky's stuff is in a bag."

"You take the pup, and I'll carry the goods. Where's your laptop case?"

Lucky followed me as I dropped the bathroom ditty bag into the suitcase and packed my laptop into its case. We were already in our boots, and I'd carried my coat up from the restaurant, so I slipped it on.

Kyle quickly checked through the room to ensure we didn't forget anything, and we headed out.

On our way down to the lobby, Luke texted Kyle's phone to say they were already in their truck and wondered if we wanted to follow them. He texted Luke, saying we did and were on our way out.

Surprisingly, most roads were snow-covered but had gotten plowed at some point, so we drove slowly. We saw several vacated vehicles in ditches covered in white. The snow had stopped falling, and the sun popped out, making the world a glittering landscape of trees, fences, barns, and homes. It took an hour to reach SPI headquarters outside any city limits in the middle of nowhere.

The long driveway had been freshly plowed, and we noticed an unfamiliar vehicle truck outside the pole barn.

"I wonder if that's Jacob's vehicle," Kyle said as he parked beside it. Max parked his truck behind us.

James had shoveled a path to the porch before we arrived and now was cleaning the snow from the porch steps. He waved and motioned us toward their house entry instead of around the side to the office door.

We hurried over as he waited by the steps.

"We got a nice fire going, and Sandy brewed a fresh pot of coffee and made some hot chocolate." He noticed Lucky in my arms. "Who you got there? Is that your newest addition, Lucky?" He stepped over, grabbed the puppy out of my arms, and held him up, saying, "Hello, little fella. You gotta go potty?" James had already cleared a little spot for the pup to use. He set Lucky on the ground, holding his leash. "I got him covered. You all get inside, and we'll be in as soon as the little dude's done with his business."

I couldn't believe how friendly and unafraid our puppy acted with everyone.

Sandy opened the door before we got to it. "Come in out of the cold. I'm so glad you all made it without incident. Jacob mentioned the roads weren't as bad as he'd anticipated."

I recognized Jacob from the Zoom meeting. He stood leaning against the wide entryway into the living room. "It's great to meet the group in person, finally." He stepped over to shake hands with all of us.

"We've all been looking forward to meeting you also." Kyle shook his hand.

"What's everyone's drink order?" Sandy headed toward the kitchen area. A half wall separated the living room from the kitchen. I followed her as the others settled onto the large sofa that circled the fireplace.

I poured the hot chocolate for Luke, Max, and me, and Sandy poured the coffee for the others. We set the steaming cups on a couple of trays and hand-delivered the last cup just as James came inside with Lucky.

"Oh my gosh, what a little cutie." Sandy hurried toward them, setting the empty trays on the half wall. "Let me see the furry little nugget." She lifted Lucky into her arms, hugged him to her cheek, and then carried him to me, dropping the pup onto my lap. "He's so dang cute."

"Well, you can't have him," I teased.

Everyone chuckled. Then Luke added, "Bri won't let anyone have that little critter, not even her best friend."

The furry runt circled my lap until he finally settled, closing his eyes.

Sandy brought over a blanket. "I noticed he's damp from the snow and probably cold too."

I wrapped it around Lucky, noticing he was shivering a bit.

Kyle grappled inside my computer case and pulled out the notebooks and pens. "You all get one of each, which will help us communicate. There's always the chance of a spirit listener." We all nodded as Kyle passed them out.

Sandy had refilled the trays, one with cookies and the other with smoky quartz crystal leather strapped necklaces and polished pocket-sized smoky crystal gemstones. "We want to make sure you are all covered with protection. Coating yourselves with sea salt mist is another precaution, and it doesn't hurt your clothing but can sometimes leave a powdery residue on your skin."

James carried in a box that contained spray bottles. "Here's the sea salt mist sprays." He set the box on the long coffee table in front of the couch next to the trays. "Each of you take one and use it every day, at least while we're dealing with this case. Sandy wrote directions on the bottles on how to mix the blend to refill it."

Kyle misted me and Lucky and then himself. The other guys did it, also. So did James and Sandy.

"Now, I think we're ready to have our meeting." James nodded. "Let's get started."

Chapter Nine

Bri

"Bri, do you have some suggestions for us?" James shoved a chair next to Sandy on the end of the couch.

I started writing like a mad dog, and then Sandy suggested the guys get the large whiteboard from the office.

"James, maybe you should also bring some of the larger smoky Crystals to set around us." Sandy rose and looked at me. "I'm going to follow them to ensure they get everything necessary for this meeting. You can hang out near the fire with Lucky. He's still shivering." She gave him a quick pat on the head. "We won't be long." Sandy hurried down the hallway to catch them before the door closed to the connecting SPI offices on the south side of their house.

"Okay, Lucky, that coffee and hot chocolate went right through me. It's my turn to go potty." I picked up the pup, left the blanket, and carried him into the bathroom. A voice bellowed through my brain as I set him on the floor.

"If you ever want to save your grandmother from the likes of me, you better agree to take her place soon. She won't be around much longer." *Whitenmeyer*.

What in the hell? He kidnapped Grams? My worst fears of where Grams went when she last left Lucky melted into thick muck. *How?* The malicious spectral retrieval was something I'd never dealt with; now, my Grams' spirit depended on me. My vision blurred, and then all the lights went out, leaving only inky black, like a moonless night in the middle of nowhere. My heart hammered like a band of bass drums.

Suddenly, Whitenmeyer stood in front of me. "Hello, gorgeous. You know what you must do for your grandmother."

A flash of Grams burst into my vision as if I were standing beside her. She appeared bruised and broken, eyes closed with tears dripping from the corners, tied to a tall cot-like bed. That picture took my breath away as that cot looked like a historic surgical bed, probably from the late 1800s.

I touched my chest, feeling the crystal there, and then automatically lifted the necklace over my head and dropped it. Then I removed the crystal stones in my pocket and dropped them. As soon as I did that, the inky black lifted. We were back inside the 1880s mansion, standing at the bottom of the staircase as if I had traveled back in time.

Beautiful young women milled about, scantily clad in undergarments or see-through dresses. Most of them had a man at their side. Some couples climbed the stairs to the rooms above or, as I noticed from the open double doors, danced to the slow music playing in the large room next to this one. Everyone sounded cheerful, but those young women's expressions told a much different story.

Whitenmeyer grabbed my arm, and I couldn't pull away as if my brain no longer controlled my body. We walked up the stairs to the top story. "That perfume you have all over your body needs removing, and I've got the perfect place for us to bathe." He stopped in the hallway long enough to scrape his nails up my arms and slither his tongue along my neck, which he withdrew immediately. *It must be the sea salt water had an effect. That must also be what he considered my perfume.* His hot breath sent chills, not the good kind. My stomach lurched, and I couldn't stop the force of the up-chuck, puking all over him.

Surprisingly, he came out unscathed, but it felt so real that I imagined it might appear on James and Sandy's bathroom floor, along with Lucky and my smoky quartz crystals.

Whitenmeyer pulled me along the hallway. I could hear what went on through the closed doors as we passed. Sometimes, the sounds were amorous, but mostly they were of vulgar rutting males or terrifying female screams of pain. I attempted to yank myself out of Whitenmeyer's grip, but my body seemed totally under his control. Like last time, my brain wasn't in charge of anything.

We stopped at the last door, which he opened and shoved me inside. I stumbled and fell, feeling like a knocked-over bowl of jelly. Nothing hurt, but it should have. I heard him walking around me, scathingly laughing and stopped a few feet away, but I couldn't turn my head to see him.

"Ileana. Your granddaughter, Bri, is here. She came thinking I would release you, but she took so long to get here; not sure I have to follow through with any deals unless Bri commits to staying." Again, the sound of his laughter disturbed me like his hot breath. My stomach lurched, and I tossed my cookies. Nothing lay before me, so I figured it went on James and Sandy's bathroom floor again.

"Bri?" Grams' trembling voice seemed amplified in my ears.

"You can respond, Bri, but your ability to move is compromised...for now." Whitenmeyer stepped back and yanked me to my feet. He held me on both sides of my waist from behind, moving me forward.

Grams studied me as I came nearer. She looked exactly like the flash picture that burst into my head when Whitenmeyer first stood in front of me. "Bri, make no promises to him," she said. Her eyes slammed shut as Whitenmeyer punched his fist into her cheek.

I was sure he had just broken her neck. "You'll never get a promise from me until you let my grandmother leave." My eyes blurred as tears rolled down my face.

"That's what I figured." Whitenmeyer wrenched me backward.

I watched as Grams' body vanished, and I hoped she went to the other side, already healed, as I had done at the hotel.

"None of your friends will be able to communicate with her. She'll end up living inside that mutt until it dies. No one will have the ability to rescue you." He dropped me onto the empty cot, grabbed a pair of scissors off a surgical tray, and then started cutting my clothes.

I closed my eyes, knowing my body would soon become a Frankensteinette.

* * *

Kyle

Before James opened the door going back into the house, Jacob crashed to the floor, and then I heard Lucky barking. "Hurry, James, let me into the house. Something's wrong. Bri would never allow Lucky to lose control of his barking." I turned toward Max. "You go check on Jacob." Max instantly rushed toward him.

James flipped the key into the lock, and I turned it, opened the door, and shoved past him. Sandy and Luke followed behind, while

James and Max stayed with Jacob. Lucky barked and scratched from the other side of the bathroom door. I tried the doorknob, and thankfully, it popped open. Lucky jumped on my legs, continuing to bark. I lifted him, handed him to Luke, and then hurried to Bri, who was lying unconscious in a puddle of vomit. I checked her pulse and breathing.

"Let me through. I've had nurse training." Sandy waved Luke out of the way. "Did you check her pulse?" she asked me.

"Yes, but I'd feel better if you checked it. Bri must have passed out from throwing up. I didn't even know she was sick." I couldn't believe she wouldn't have told me she'd felt bad. And staring at the mess on the floor, I couldn't believe she had that much in her stomach. Then I realized her crystal necklace and the gemstones she'd carried in her pockets were part of the pile on the floor. "She was so afraid of falling asleep that she barely ate anything this morning. There shouldn't be that much in her stomach. Plus, her protection crystals are on the floor. Something made her remove them, and maybe a threat forced her to comply?"

Sandy looked up at me. "I'm thinking the same thing, Kyle."

Just then, Jacob came to the door, holding a notebook that said, 'Whitenmeyer is listening to our conversations but can't see anything – only hears for now. Bri's grandmother is residing inside me.' He raised his brows and nodded in confirmation.

"How in the heck did that happen?" Then I raised my hand for him not to tell me. "I'm glad you're okay, Jacob. I'll be out in a minute after we figure out what to do with Bri." Having Bri's grandmother back would give us a better idea of what we can expect moving forward with a plan, but I suspected that Bri stayed with Whitenmeyer so Grams could leave. And I was sure Grams didn't go on her terms, but Whitenmeyer's.

"I've got some clothes Bri could wear if you want to change them for her. Or I can." Sandy stood up. "I'll get a mop and clean the floor and her crystals. Do you want to bathe her? We have a bathroom off from our bedroom upstairs and to the left that you're welcome to use."

"Sandy, that would be perfect. We spent last night at a hotel where Max and Luke stayed, so she had extra clothes in a suitcase inside the SUV. I'll ask Luke to grab that for me." I glanced down at Bri. "Maybe I should clean her face before I carry her across the room and up the stairs." I was sure the group would be in the living room by now. "The last time she returned from something like this, I had put that crystal necklace on her."

Sandy opened a cupboard door and grabbed a washcloth. She stuck it under the faucet for a few seconds and squeezed out some water. "Here you go." She handed it to me, rescued the crystals, and washed them while I wiped off Bri's face. "Here are the crystals. I'll grab the mop, and you can move her upstairs. After you bathe her, there are a couple of spare bedrooms across the hall from ours. Go ahead and lay her in one of them for now." She stood directly in front of me and mouthed: "Until we figure out how to awaken her if those crystals don't work."

I quickly slipped the necklace over Bri's head to prove to Sandy that Bri would awaken. We both waited, staring at Bri. Her eyes never opened, which meant Whitenmeyer figured out a way to get around the power of the crystal. *What in the hell spectral type were we dealing with?*

Hopefully, Grams could communicate through Jacob what we must do to get Bri back. The thought of Bri's soul held captive someplace other than inside her body made me question all the people who lay in hospital beds in commas. *What if something similar happened to them? A madman spectral could confiscate their souls and then abuse them?*

The gang watched as I carried Bri across the room toward the stairs. Jacob nodded, lifting the notebook and mouthing, 'Hurry.'

"Luke, would you mind bringing the suitcase in from the SUV? I need a change of clothes for Bri. Just bring it upstairs."

"I'm on it." Luke jumped up and ran for the door.

The fear on everyone's face didn't ease my worry as I carried Bri up the steps. Her bath went fast. Considering her unconscious state, I dressed her as quickly as possible and laid her on a bed in the spare room closest to the stairs. I ran down the steps and realized the meeting had begun without me, which gave me instant relief. "So, what's happening? Catch me up so we can continue."

Jacob tilted his head toward the whiteboard filled with words. "The best way to catch up is to read this." He pointed out a couple of ideas. One was performing a dark magic ritual of forcing the entity to Mother Earth, which I knew Bri would never agree to use dark magic. Another was to call in the light, which sounded more like a force Bri had worked with previously. But Whitenmeyer had a lot of years of evil before he became an entity. Our research started in his early childhood. I wondered if there was any way to redeem his soul. Right now, every thought inside my head screamed, destroy the beast to free Bri's soul.

Chapter Ten

Bri

I felt nothing.

When Whitenmeyer had me before, he had created a lot of pain-rendering torture, and I could feel all of it. But this time, my body didn't respond to anything. Something had changed, and I wasn't sure what protected me from his torture.

I sat in an enormous claw bathtub filled with water, so must have fallen asleep as I didn't recall when or how I got from the surgery cot into the tub. I did remember a feminine voice. The woman had given me some water, maybe some food, and put something on me to take away the pain. Her face never came to my mind, like perhaps I never opened my eyes.

Steam rose in wispy curls from the surface, making it appear more like staring through fog. I realized Whitenmeyer sat across from me, but he didn't come across like his horror-story self. He looked much younger than in his photos and more muscular than a doctor. His face had changed from the crazed evil man with pointy teeth into an attractive gentleman.

"How did you come to be here, at Whitenmeyer Manor?" he asked with an aristocratic English accent.

I wanted to say, 'from you,' and attempted to say it, but I had no voice and wasn't sure if my lips moved. I watched through the mist as Whitenmeyer's hand slid up my right calf, and his fingers rubbed behind my knee.

"You feel very slender, and your skin is so soft." He studied me, making me uncomfortable.

Glancing around the room, without moving my head, I looked for an escape route but didn't see a door or any clothes, only a bed and a couple of rolled towels. I wanted to remove Whitenmeyer's hand, but my arms weren't responding. Was I drugged? Water filled my eyes and emptied, only to refill again, but I felt nothing on my face. How could I sense this man's hand and not tears dripping down my cheeks?

"A lot of the women here are mute. Are you? Can you nod or shake your head for a yes or no response?" His smile seemed genuine as if he cared. He waited a moment, then said, "My name is Lyndor. Lyndor Whitenmeyer. I am a cousin to Leo, the owner of this establishment. It's my first visit here, and Leo recommended you as a good match for me." He smiled again, but something in how his brows drew inward made me think he might have some concern for me.

He leaned forward, his fingers curled around my upper arms and pulled me into his chest. "Is this your first time with a man?"

I closed my eyes and thought of Kyle, wishing the beating heart against my ear belonged to him. Lyndor seemed like a kind man, but he wasn't Kyle. I'd already given my heart, body, and soul to Kyle. I kept my eyes closed, believing what happened was only a made-up dream and that the man sitting in the tub with me was Kyle...only Kyle...always Kyle.

* * *

Kyle

I wrote my notes to the group, 'Is this information coming from Bri's grandmother? I don't think Bri would want us to use dark magic. That's why I ask.'

Jacob turned and wrote, 'Kyle, it is Ileana, Bri's grandmother. I'm not anxious to use dark magic, either. But Whitenmeyer is an all-dark spirit, and those need different treatment to bring them back to the light. His only way back might happen by using a dark magic ritual. Bri's soul is gone. We need to get her back before we can't get her back. She'll be lost to us and won't know who we are. Time becomes warped in the spirit realm. Minutes here are hours there. Give Jacob access to my journal so he understands what comes next. I will guide him, but it helps if he knows what to expect.' Jacob turned from the whiteboard, glanced around the room, and then focused on me. "I see my message and will follow through." Then he returned to the whiteboard and wrote, 'But, I'm okay with my body guided to do or say the right things.' He turned toward the group and added, "Just sayin'."

"Okay, we have a little research to do." Luke stood. He flipped his notebook and went to the center of the room for all of us to see. 'Let's get our girl back.'

"I'm going to check on Bri and get the journal from her suitcase." I raced up the steps to the bedroom, quickly crossing the room to see her lovely face. The only thing on her body that moved was Bri's eyelids fluttering, even though her eyes remained closed. "Bri, we need you, babe. Please come back." I kissed her lips, which were cold like death. I got on the bed, shuffling beneath the covers to wrap my arms around her. She felt like ice, even though she didn't shiver.

"Hey, how's our girl?" Luke stepped into the room.

"I think I need to warm her up. She feels as cold as death."

Luke walked around the bed and touched her face. "Oh, my Gods. Is she breathing? Oh, I see her eyes fluttering." Luke took a heavy breath. "Best way to warm a body is skin to skin, and you know that's true."

"I'm going to stay with her for a while. I'm torn between helping with the plan or keeping her body stable. For now, I will remain up here until I can get her warmed up. Check the closet for more blankets, would you?"

Luke trotted across the room to the walk-in closet and returned with two warm-looking blankets. He unfolded and spread them across the top of the bed. "I'll close the door, and you do what you must. We need her back with us. I'll let everyone know you'll watch over her for a while. I know they all will understand. We got your back, Kyle. Just stay with her."

"Wait. Before you go, grab the journal inside the suitcase over there." I pointed. "Jacob needs that."

Luke got it and headed toward the door.

"What's going on up here?" Max stood at the open doorway. "Is she doing all right?" He stared at Luke as he approached. "Do we need to help?" Max's eyes never left Luke.

"Nope, Kyle's got this. We're needed downstairs to finish our meeting." Luke nodded his head and tilted it toward the hallway. "We won't be expecting you anytime soon, Kyle."

"Call us if you need anything." Max turned and left with Luke.

They chatted down the hall, and their heavy footsteps shuffled down the stairs. It seemed like a vacuum afterward. Dead silence, a freezing body, and barely a breath came from Bri. I quickly undressed her and then climbed out of bed long enough to undress. Slipping back underneath all those covers, I drew the back side of Bri's body against me with my arms and legs wrapped around her, hugging her soft, slender body into mine. My eyes closed, and I tried to shut my mind off what might be happening to her in the spirit world. I whispered in her ear, "I love you, Bri Lancaster, and I'm coming to get you back."

* * *

Bri

I didn't know how long Lyndor held me in the tub, but when I finally opened my eyes, the steam from the water had dissipated. Lyndor's body shivered, and his forearms had goosebumps. I lifted my head to look at him. His lips appeared purple. I still couldn't talk, or could I? I had just lifted my head, so I tried, "You are cold." My words came out like a whisper, but he heard me.

"You can speak." He gently hugged his face to mine. "Let's get out of here." He stood with me in his arms. "Can you stand?"

"I think so," I whispered.

He allowed my feet to drop onto the floor but still held me until I became balanced. "I'll grab a towel for you." He strutted across the room to the bed where the rolled towels lay, wrapping one around his waist, and then hurried back with one for me. "You're quite a beautiful woman. I'm so sorry that I've made you sad."

"I don't belong here," still whispering, I wrapped the towel around me. "I'm from another time and place."

Lyndor stared at me as if I'd lost my mind.

And I must have lost it to think anyone here would believe what I had just stated. *How stupid!* I stared at the floor, standing before him and not knowing what came next. A thousand questions drilled through my brain, wondering if I'd just lost the one man who seemed like a negotiable person. Someone that might even help me escape the monster's lair.

"I'm wondering if you were drugged, Mistress. How are you feeling now?" His lips pinched together as he felt my forehead, then he dropped his head and placed his ear between my breasts. "Your heart seems steady, but maybe a little fast because of our situation here, naked under wraps." He softly chuckled and then glanced at my face. "Please, excuse my rudeness. Like I mentioned, I've never been to a brothel before. I'm nervous I will not perform as I should for a woman, especially one as lovely and conscientious as yourself." He gathered my hands in his. "Come, let's get warm underneath the covers. I will not do anything you do not want me to. I'll happily hold you for warmth if that works for you."

His kindness overwhelmed me. *Why would Whitenmeyer place me with someone other than himself? Especially someone as kind as Lyndor.* "Thank you for your kindness, Mister Whitenmeyer. I am cold, and the warmth of the bed would help."

He pulled the covers back and then quickly removed his towel. He turned toward me, reaching for the top of my towel. I knew I needed to play the part and allowed him to take it as I stared at the ceiling. His breath sucked in, and I could sense his eyes roving my body.

I quickly dove under the covers, moving to the other side of the bed. Lyndor took his time climbing onto the bed on his hands and knees, crawling to me on top of the bedspread. His face hovered over mine as his hands and knees parted, each taking a side of my covered body. I closed my eyes, knowing what came next. I felt the tears fleeing to the edges of my face and into my ears.

Lyndor kissed my eyelids and gently licked away my tears. "I will only do what you allow me to do."

"Will you get under the covers and hold me? Only hold me. Please. Nothing more." *What man would do that?* He was naked, for Goddesses" sake. And so was I. *What in the hell was I thinking?* That he would hold my naked body against his naked body and do nothing?

He crawled under the covers, turned me away, and pulled my backside into his body. The heat of his hardness burned against my buttocks, feeling like Kyle. His warm breath against my neck also felt like Kyle's. I closed my eyes and clasped my hands over his as he planted them on my breasts. Exactly what Kyle always did with his hot palms, and a sudden warmth climbed through my whole body. I knew Kyle held me...somewhere. Kyle had me just like this.

* * *

Kyle

Bri's body warmed against mine, and I couldn't stop the building erection from happening. She always knew how to turn me on. *Maybe having sex could bring her back to me.* Her breathing changed first slow and deep breaths, then picking up. I touched her breasts the way she liked and her backside pressed against me. I slid one hand down to her sweet spot and got a moan from her that turned me into a rock-hard stallion. I parted her legs, and she moved her body back farther to accommodate me, helping guide me with her hands, which told me that I had her in spirit and body.

"Yes, Kyle, yes...," she murmured.

And back from the spirit realm, she came to me in a wild orgasm, leaving me wanting even more of her.

"You're back." I held her close, kissing her shoulder and cheek, and finally flipped her over and kissed her lips.

"I love you, Kyle Benton. You have no idea how happy I am to find myself in your arms." And she kissed me, over and over, until I realized she was crying. "I knew you were with me," she sighed as tears rolled down her face. "Thank you for not leaving me alone. I needed you, and you were there. And now, I am here."

I had no idea what she meant by that, but I would find out later after we had more of each other.

Chapter Eleven

Bri

Awakening in Kyle's arms went beyond expectations, but it happened as if in a dream or by magic. I had closed my eyes, imagining until I genuinely believed Kyle lay with me, skin to skin, breath to breath, and heartbeat to heartbeat. Then I awoke next to him. But where were we? I slid from his warmth to sit up and look around, noticing my smoky crystal necklace against my chest. I understood that it might have contributed to my spirit returning.

"Bri?" Kyle moved to sit beside me. "You're back, but I'm unsure how it happened."

"I think this helped." I showed him the crystal.

"I put it back on you, but you didn't return like before." His arm went around me as I leaned into him. "Why did you take it off?"

"To save Grams. But I don't know for sure that happened, and how would anyone know?" My eyes welled, but I refused to become emotional. I needed answers and slipped out of bed to find them. Nothing appeared familiar in the room except our open suitcase on the floor. "Where are we?" I bent down to grab Grams' journal I'd packed.

"We're still at James and Sandy's house in one of their upstairs spare bedrooms. And you're not going to find what I think you're after. Luke took it downstairs."

I stepped to the window and spread the curtains enough to peek outside. Snow. It had started falling again, coming down like a total white-out.

"I don't have a notebook up here if you know what I mean." Kyle rustled out of bed. "There's a meeting going on right now."

I turned and studied Kyle, whose striking blue eyes seemed to slowly sweep every inch of me, making me feel as exposed yet horny as ever while his naked chiseled body swaggered toward me.

He wrapped his arms around me, kissing my ear, and whispered, "Jacob, not Lucky, has a spirit guide."

* * *

We settled on the end of the half-circle sofa in front of the fireplace. My face heated as the SPI team stared at Kyle and me, making me wonder if they'd heard any of our commotion in the upstairs bedroom. Lucky jumped out of Sandy's arms and ran to us, attempting to hop onto my lap. I pulled him up.

"Hello, little man. Am I happy to see you."

"Not as happy as we are to see you," Jacob said, standing before the group next to the whiteboard. "I was so afraid for you."

Even though the voice was Jacob's, I knew Grams spoke through him. I handed Lucky off to Kyle and ran to Jacob, giving him a big hug. "And I was so afraid for you." When I realized the hug didn't get reciprocated, I stepped back.

Jacob's cheeks and ears turned bright red as he stood like a fence post, hands to his sides with his body shaking. After a moment of silence, while everyone watched him, he finally said, "I think our friend just left the building. Something like a flood flushed through my whole body and then suddenly vanished. I think she's..." His eyes rolled back, and I half-caught him as he fell into me. At least I kept his head from hitting the floor.

James, Luke, and Max rushed over. Kyle stood right behind me. They moved Jacob to the couch, and Sandy draped a blanket over him.

I didn't move, reading everything Jacob had written on the whiteboard. Grams had come up with two possibilities for getting Whitenmeyer to rest in peace. I grabbed a notebook and pen and wrote down everything listed.

Kyle took a picture of it on his phone. "In case we need a backup." He smiled at me. "We're a team, after all."

"Looks like," I pointed at the whiteboard listing several different crystal gemstones, "we need to check that supply room and make sure we have all the necessities required to get the job done." Talking without telling everything got old fast, but so far, the team seemed to pick up every meaning implied.

"I've got that list," Max and Luke said simultaneously. They grinned at each other. "We got this and will return with everything we need," Luke stated.

"Let's grab our coats before we take on the snowstorm." Max headed toward the coat hooks next to the outside door.

"I'm going with you." Sandy followed. "That will save some time accumulating it all. We can load it directly into the van parked inside the pole barn next to the supply room."

James walked over to Kyle and me. "Let's settle on the couch and see what you have to tell us, Bri." He pointed at the notebook in my hand. "I'll grab us another coffee."

I set my notebook and pen down and followed James into the kitchen.

"Don't you want to get started?" He looked at me and mimicked writing.

"No one knows how I make my coffee."

He laughed. "Yea, we do. An almost full cup of milk, a splash of coffee, and warm it up in the microwave. Does that sound about right?"

My mouth dropped open. "Yes. Wow. I had no idea anyone paid attention."

"We've all talked about it behind your back." He chuckled again. "Nothing offensive, just something we've all noted."

I nodded and smiled, then walked back to the couch and wrote until my fingers cramped, leaving nothing out, especially Lyndor Whitenmeyer. I wanted to know more about him as it might be useful if I ever revisited the mansion in spirit form. By how Jacob described his flushed-out feeling, I added that Grams might have been retaken. Hard to say where Grams actually went as she would go in and out of Lucky without notice, and I never found out why she left, where she went, or how she got back.

I handed the notebook to Kyle. "Here you go. It's everything I can think of right now. I will run Lucky outside and grab my laptop to research Lyndor Whitenmeyer, Leonard's cousin."

James scooched closer to Kyle so they could read the pages together.

I headed for the hooks in the entryway, where my coat hung. Lucky followed. I hooked the pup to the leash, then shoved my arms into my coat sleeves, zipping it, and headed outside. Lucky and I walked across the porch to the south side of the house, where James had cleared a space for the pup to potty. He squatted and peed. The snowflakes were the biggest I'd ever seen, and the cleared area needed some hefty shoveling, as did the sidewalk and the driveway. We trudged through it to retrieve my laptop, and I grabbed a couple of puppy toys. "Let's go, little dude." Considering the weather, we hurried as fast as possible and had to brush off a lot of snow from Lucky and me before entering the house.

Kyle and James lifted their heads when I walked inside. I couldn't read their expressions, but I sensed their feelings. Compassion and fear struck me like a shield pushing me back, and then a knife striking my heart. I shrugged off my coat but left the leash on Lucky so he wouldn't wander off.

"Bri, why didn't you tell me what Whitenmeyer had done to you?" Kyle walked over.

"You know we can't talk about it, right?" I stared at Kyle and then glanced at James. "You know what you need to, right?" I pointed at the notebook James still held in his hand.

"Yes, we know a lot right now. Let's wait for Jacob to awaken before we go any further." James rose from the couch and walked into the kitchen. "I'm going to make some BLTs for a late lunch. You go ahead and research." He nodded at me and began pulling things from the fridge and cupboards. "Cozy up to the fire. I just stoked it."

"I can help you with lunch, James." Kyle left me on the couch with my laptop and Lucky while he went to help James.

My fingers ran across the keyboard, tapping in Lyndor Whitenmeyer, mid-to-late 1800s, Southwest Michigan, for any research information. I knew Luke had mad skills for this kind of research, although he had yet to find his birth father. That seemed an ongoing investigation for Max and Luke between culinary training classes and chef interning at my father's restaurants.

Luke, Max, Kyle, and me had all done research to find Luke's birth father because his mother hadn't told anyone of her pregnancy before marrying the man who *thought* he was Luke's real father. Then his supposed "real" father had to take a blood test, and it showed no matches to Luke's gene pool. His mother had passed away years ago, never telling anyone about the possibility that someone else could be Luke's real dad—quite the conundrum and an ongoing investigation for all of us.

Nothing showed up for Lyndor Whitenmeyer, so I decided to wait for any suggestions from Luke when he came back with Max and Sandy.

The aroma of frying bacon spread into the living room, making my stomach growl. Sandy, Luke, and Max entered the entryway with a giant burst of freezing air. They all removed their coats, hats, and gloves. Sandy held a small velvet bag filled with something and carefully set it on a shelf.

"Holy hell, it's another blasted snowstorm outside." Max stepped into the kitchen with Luke and Sandy right behind. "Wow, that smells good."

"Everything is almost ready." James and Kyle were loading plates and bowls with everything needed for the sandwiches so everyone could make their own. "We can either sit around the counter or grab a plate and head closer to the warm fireplace." James pointed at the fixings on the counter. The guys all lined up to load a plate.

Sandy headed my way with the little bag back in her hand. "I have something else we should all keep on our person." She opened the bag and dropped a polished black gemstone into my palm. "Black Tourmaline."

I sensed its energy immediately. "This is another stone for," I lifted my head and moved my lips, 'protection from negative energies.'

Her eyes widened, and she smiled. "Yes, very good. You always impress me with your knowledge, Bri."

"And you impress me with your wisdom, Sandy." I quickly held the stone between my palms to get a good feel of the stone's energy surging through me. "Perfect." I slipped it into my pocket.

"Come on, girls. Let's eat." James waved us over.

I stopped next to Jacob. His brows creased together as if he were suffering from pain.

Sandy stood beside me and touched his forehead. "He's as pale as a sheet and is covered in a cold sweat."

"That's not good." I considered what was likely happening with Jacob's spirit. "He's getting tortured." I pulled the stone from my pocket, dropped it into one of his hands, and curled his fingers around it. Sandy dropped another one into his other hand and did the same with his fingers. We wrapped our fingers around Jacob's, and then Sandy and I held hands for a three-way connection. I closed my eyes, took a couple of deep breaths, and said, "I am filled with love and light. The Divine is my shield." When I repeated it, Sandy joined in, and by the third time, James, Luke, Max, and Kyle joined us.

I opened my eyes to see Jacob's lips repeating the words we had just said. "Everybody connect hands to form a circle and repeat the mantra three times. Close your eyes and think about Jacob opening his eyes and coming back to us." I squeezed Kyle's hand and started again, "I am filled with love and light. The Divine is my shield." We all repeated it, and by the third time, I heard Jacob's voice joining in. I opened my eyes to see a big smile on his face. Kyle helped him sit up on the couch.

"Holy hell, what is that smell? It's like heaven." He glanced around the room. "Is that bacon?"

James chuckles. "Yes, let's eat. Then we'll want to know where you've been, young man."

Chapter Twelve

Bri

After lunch, while everyone carried their empty plates into the kitchen, Luke pulled me aside. "Good, Gods, Bri, were you abused and tortured by that crazed, maniac, evil one every time you passed out?"

I raised my forefinger to my lips and shook my head. I quickly set my plate in the sink and grasped Luke's hand, leading him back to the couch. I grabbed my pen and pad of paper, then wrote, 'Pretty much, but this time I didn't feel anything as if my nerves had gotten shut off, nor could I talk or move my lips. And then, halfway through my time on the other side, my voice and sensitivities came back. I want to know more about Lyndor Whitenmeyer.' I looked at Luke and then mouthed: "Lyndor is nothing like Leonard."

"You've got an internet deep-search pro standing here, woman." Luke grinned. "I'll grab my laptop and research some of those players for us. Be right back." Luke headed for the door, grabbing his coat off the hook on the way outside.

Sandy handed out a black tourmaline gemstone to Kyle and then to James.

"Everyone else already has one. You boys must carry that one with your other stone, either on a leather thong around your neck or in your pocket."

"Thanks, Sandy." Kyle slid onto the couch beside Lucky and me. "How are you doing? Have you found anything more about what you're researching?"

"Not really, but Luke is..." Just as I was answering Kyle, Luke barged inside the entryway. He looked like a snowman with blowing wind and snowflakes following him into the small foyer until he finally shut the door. "Oh, my gosh. Get your buns over here to get warmed up." I scootched toward Kyle so Luke could settle closer to the fireplace.

As soon as he sat, he flipped open his laptop and tapped away on the keys. "We'll get some answers, don't worry."

Jacob stepped to the side of the couch, peering over Luke's shoulder. "Oh, man, that's a great site. No matter what you ask, there's always a response; if not firsthand, it gives you another link for the answer."

Kyle cozied beside me to watch Luke's magic fingers in action. Max stood behind the couch, watching Luke's screen. We were quite the huddle. Even James and Sandy wandered over beside Max. I could tell Luke loved every minute of the attention as his fingers raced over the keys. Then he stopped. Lyndor's face filled the screen.

"He's an actor from Chicago and the number one male actor in plays performed in Chicago and New York City. Swoon-worthy for both women and men; the women want him, and the men want to be him."

I studied the pictures that Luke scrolled through and realized Lyndor had played the 'gentleman' role with me, every minute with him like an unfolding play. He might have come across as a gentleman, but his vile evilness blindsided the innocent. Lyndor gained those women's trust, compassion, and empathy. Then he sprang like a guileful sharp-toothed jackal, robbing everything personal and loving by a guiltless rape in the guise of something more meaningful—only an empty shell of a woman left behind, struggling to surface from his tumultuous wake. I suddenly realized, Lyndor had climbed the ladder of heinous evil, even topping Leonard's brutal ways.

I patted Luke's arm to get his attention and mouthed: "Are Lyndor and Leonard co-owners of the mansion prostitution business?"

Luke typed a bit more, and another screen popped up. He enlarged it. "Looks like some sort of contract." He pointed at the two signatures on the bottom. "Interesting."

"I just looked up the weather app on my phone. We're in for snow the rest of the day and night. Do we want to attempt a trip tonight or wait until tomorrow night?"

"What if we..." I stopped.

Sandy tapped my shoulder and finished with, "Perform something here?"

I nodded. Most everyone's mouths dropped open as I glanced around the group. "It's worth a try. For whatever reason, there's power building by waiting." I could sense it tap against me, pressing on my shield of protection.

James stepped around the couch to stand in front of us. "Sandy and Bri, you set up a drawing with details so we know what else to bring inside...unless we want to use the pole barn space?" James raised a brow and looked at me.

"That sounds like a good plan...the pole barn." That way, we would be closer to everything we needed to pull off a ritual, sending those two men to mother earth so she could clean them up and release them into the light realm.

"I'll keep researching. Maybe we'll learn something we can use." Luke tilted his head and winked.

"Jacob, Max, Kyle, and I can start clearing an area of the pole barn. You ladies, go ahead with your whiteboard layout. Someone will retrieve it when you've finished." James glanced at the guys and motioned toward the entryway. "Let's scoot. Luke, good hunting to you." He gave a little salute toward Luke and then followed the guys, grabbing coats and heading out.

Sandy turned the whiteboard around. "Here you go." She mouthed: "Label everything so I can make a running list. I can snap a picture to get the layout so we won't need to take the whiteboard to the barn."

I nodded, drawing a large circle, and laying out smaller circles for the smoky quartz crystal stones of protection. Sandy added tinier circles for the black tourmaline, and I added a few larger circles of amethyst stones for stability and healing should something go array. I added a sea salt and lavender trail to enclose the loop, keeping the evil entities inside the circle like a trap. I made a list of white tapered candles and lighters for everyone and made a note to find a good mantra that calls to mother earth for assistance.

I stood back and looked over the drawing. "Feels like I'm missing something." I thought about the properties of specific quartz crystals and gemstones as I turned to Sandy. "I need to research, but it might help if I checked your supply of stones. Would you mind if I walked through the warehouse to see what's available?"

"I'll go with you." Sandy held up a notebook and pen. "If you have certain preferences for a stone's properties, I might be able to help with that."

I nodded, realizing Sandy's knowledge went relatively high regarding the properties of specific stones. She would know what I wanted exactly. We made a good team that way. I quickly shrugged into my coat, grabbed Lucky with his leash still attached, and headed outside. Sandy followed me.

Lucky trotted off in the direction of his potty place.

"You go dewater the pup, and I'll check on the guys. Then you and I can get started with our set-up."

* * *

The guys had cleaned out a huge space for our ritual. The set-up would go fast. A lot of the materials we would use had gotten unloaded from the van they filled earlier and now stood close to the cleared area. Jacob drew a good-sized blue chalk circle on the concrete floor so we could start placing the items for the ritual. James must have put a couple of heaters closer because it no longer felt like a snowstorm outside.

Kyle had walked outside to grab Lucky's box so the pup had a place to rest with his blanket. He placed it close to the warehouse doorway, where Lucky could see us but be far enough away to relax.

When Jacob finished the chalk circle, he walked over to me. "We haven't had a chance to talk much." He reached out his hand to shake mine, and I received a little shock when our hands touched.

"Sorry about that. Not sure how come I hold static." I giggled a second as I waved my hand in the air as if that would get rid of the static electricity. "We're old friends, in a spiritual way, Jacob." I smiled. "I've never met anyone else who can see ghosts and communicate with them like I do. I'm so happy you're part of our team."

"Well, I can see them, but not sure that I communicate with them well. My initial instinct is to run in the opposite direction." He chuckled. "I'm excited to learn more about spirit communications, and sure they have a lot to teach us."

"Well, if you haven't hung around ghosts long enough to hold a full conversation with them, maybe you *can* talk to them and hear their responses...you just haven't stuck around long enough yet." I liked Jacob; he was seemingly genuine, truthful about his experiences, and unafraid of honesty. "I'd like you to stand beside me for the ritual and follow my lead. You should be able to..." I mouthed: "See the ghosts and determine if they are virtuous or evil." I waited for his response, and when he didn't, I mouthed: "Did you share with the guys what happened while you were in the spirit realm?"

Jacob shook his head. "Would rather not."

I thought his response odd but didn't want to pressure him just in case he had gotten tortured and didn't want to relive it or had a sexual experience he didn't want to make public. I studied him for a moment, noticing the color of his eyes seemed darker.

"Did you have something else you wanted to say?" His friendly smile sharply turned villainous and then sprang back to congenial so fast I wondered if I'd imagined it.

Kyle walked up behind me and scared the crap out of me. Jacob's smile repertoire replayed toward me as Kyle's arms coiled around my waist and hugged my body into his.

A flash of the terror I'd felt while in the spirit realm, with Leonard as he prepared to torture me, washed through my body, and left me weak and shaken.

"Hey, you're trembling. Bri, is everything all right?" Kyle stepped from behind me, glanced at Jacob, and then at me.

"Guess I'm a little unsteady." I shook my head. "Not sure why?" Then I looked at Jacob, who stood quietly with that wicked, odd smile, which completely vanished when Kyle glimpsed at him. I had a terrible feeling that when Grandma flushed out of Jacob, someone had taken her place.

"Come here. Let's go sit for a minute." Kyle walked me to the other side of the building behind a parked van, where we were alone.

When we got out of earshot, I snuggled up to Kyle and whispered, "Something's off with Jacob. I think he's possessed."

Kyle backed up and stared at me. "You're kidding."

I shook my head. "I'm getting a vibe from him that I can't shake. I think Leonard is inside Jacob."

Just then, Jacob stumbled around the van. "Did someone just mention my name?" His words slurred as if he'd been drinking alcohol.

Kyle yanked me behind him. "Are you talking about the name Jacob or Leonard?"

Jacob's face twisted into a bitter mask of hatred. "Bri, you tricked me, and now your grandmother will pay with her soul. You know how to reach me. In the meantime, I'm taking more insurance."

I peeked over Kyle's shoulder in time to watch Jacob's fist strike Kyle's face. His head snapped back and caught my chin. I fell back as Kyle toppled on top of me. Jacob also fell to the ground. I crawled out from under Kyle. Both guys appeared knocked out. I shook Kyle. No response.

"Max, James," I yelled. They came running with Sandy following.

"What happened?" James placed two fingers on the side of Kyle's neck and then on Jacob's. "They're unconscious. Why?" He looked at me as if expecting answers.

So, I shared my thoughts that Leonard had possessed Jacob, even though Jacob had carried those stones of protection. And that I believed Leonard just kidnapped Kyle's spirit.

Max's mouth dropped open. "You're kidding. Why would he do that? To what gain? This whole kidnapping thing is turning into a goat rodeo." Max began pacing back and forth beside Jacob and Kyle's prone bodies. He stopped and stared at James. "What the hell is going on with this Leonard guy? Why is he kidnapping souls? How can we stop him?"

"He wants me." I dropped to my knees beside Kyle. Anger swept through me, making me want to scream as a tear of defeat slid down my cheek. "He took Kyle to get to me. Somehow, Leonard marked me as his, and I honestly don't know what that means other than he expects me to stay with him at the mansion."

Chapter Thirteen

Kyle

I opened my eyes and looked around as far as my head could turn. I lay on a high surface in a semi-dark, unfamiliar room, realizing I was no longer at James and Sandy's place. But was I unconscious there? Bri had been several times, and her spirit had left her body during those periods.

I freaked for a moment. My neck, arms, legs, and chest couldn't move. Bound to a cot with a white blanket covering my body, I couldn't tell what held me there. I attempted to yell for help, but my voice refused to work, and neither did my arms or legs. Jacob had punched me, and I went down like a lead-filled balloon. Then I wondered if I'd taken out Bri on my way to the floor of the pole barn.

My head wouldn't move much as I glanced around the room again.

Jacob.

His naked body hung on the wall with antique metal bindings on his neck, waist, wrists, and ankles. Two rods that looked like black iron were driven into the wall underneath his armpits, holding his body level. I couldn't turn my head far enough to know if his feet were on or above the floor.

I attempted to call his name to no avail. Like a sealed cave, no sound came out of my mouth. I noticed Jacob's eyes fluttered, probably in the throes of a nightmare.

Holy hell, I knew where we were—in the mansion with the devil during the late 1800s.

Why would Leonard pin Jacob to the wall...naked?

* * *

Bri

Luke got called away from his research inside the house to come to the pole barn. He helped Max and James cart Kyle and Jacob on a gurney into the house, one at a time. Because the stairs going up or down a level to the bedrooms proved too challenging, their unconscious bodies lay on the semi-circle couch, one on each end. I checked Kyle to see if he had his stones in his pocket. James checked Jacob's. Both had a smoky quartz crystal and a black tourmaline stone in their pocket. We left them there.

"I don't understand why these protective stones aren't shielding us. What can we do differently to protect ourselves?"

James looked at me wide-eyed. "Can we talk now?"

"To be honest, I'm not a hundred percent sure. But when Leonard *could* hear me and my conversations, I felt a sensitivity I no longer can feel. I believe Leonard used too much of his power, and his energy level has depleted. That had to take a lot for him to reside inside Jacob and then kidnap him and Kyle simultaneously, right after he had kidnapped Grams." I covered Kyle with the blanket hanging on top of the couch. Sandy grabbed a blanket from the opposite end and did the same for Jacob.

I glanced around the room at everyone, realizing Lucky was still in the pole barn. "Oh, my gosh, I forgot the little guy. I'll be right back." I shoved my arms into my coat and ran to the pole barn. Lucky stood on the inside of the door as I opened it. "Oh, buddy, I'm so sorry." He jumped up, dragging the leash still attached to his collar, attempting to get in my arms until I leaned down.

"I thought you'd forgotten your puppy."

"Grams? Oh my gosh, you're back." I hugged Lucky. "Oh, I need your help to get Kyle and Jacob back. How can we get Leonard out of that house, and his cousin, Lyndor?"

"Leonard used every bit of his power to take over Jacob and even more to kidnap him and Kyle. With all his energy gone, I could escape. We must hit him soon before he can amp up his power."

I swear Lucky smiled. "Grams, you have no idea how happy I am that you're back with us. We need more ideas on how to stay protected from that madman."

"Let's go talk with the others. There's no way Leonard will hear you now without his energy. He's just a plain ghost, and that, my dear, is the best time to take him out."

"What about Lyndor?" I slipped Lucky onto the ground, grabbed his leash so it didn't drag behind, and headed toward the SUV.

"Oh, yes, you spent some time with him. He's more of a monster than Leonard, snaring innocent women with his gentlemanly manner. Did you get sucked into his act?" Lucky's head cocked to the side as if Grams waited for a response.

I opened the back door of the SUV for Lucky's food and water dishes, then headed toward his potty spot. "I did but didn't figure him out until Luke found some information about him being a trendy actor and a cad for abusing unsuspecting women."

Luke poked his head out of the front door. "Hey, everything all right with Lucky?"

"Yea, I just wanted to get some of his stuff out of the SUV, and he needed to go potty. We'll be right in."

Luke had waited just inside the door and took Lucky when we came in. "Kyle and Jacob don't look so good. Their eyes are going crazy under their eyelids. I can't imagine what they must be going through right now."

"Well, guess who's returned to help us get our guys back where they belong and then send those Whitenmeyer bastards to mother earth?"

Luke's mouth dropped open a moment, then his eyes lit up. "Your grams?"

"None other. And Grams is primed to take him out as soon as possible while Leonard's energy is gone, which means he can't listen in on our conversations."

"Well, what about Lyndor?" Luke led Lucky into the kitchen, where Sandy, James, and Max sat at the counter. "Hey, everybody, Grams is back." Luke grinned with two thumbs up.

The small crowd applauded. "Thank goodness you're here, Grams. We've hit a wall with this evil spirit." Sandy looked at me and tipped her head toward Lucky, sitting on the floor beside her barstool. "Is she residing in him or you?"

"Lucky. But I can pass on all Grams' information. She wants us to work fast while the Whitenmeyers are out of commission. Well, at least Leonard is, and honestly, I'm not sure how much power Lyndor wields."

"I don't know about Lyndor. He never exposed any power. I want to talk about the setup in the pole barn. The sea salt and lavender trail around the ritual circle is perfect, but I suggest everyone also carries a sea-salt water spray bottle to help keep them inside the circle. Of course, everyone have a white taper candle lit and ready. And

I'll devise the perfect ritual mantra to call in mother earth," Grams stated. "We're in luck if we can do it tonight. There's a full moon. Also, don't forget to smudge with the white sage before starting the ceremony, all of you."

I grabbed Lucky off the floor, pulled my stool a short distance from the counter, and climbed onto it with Lucky on my lap. I explained to the group what Grams had shared.

Then Grams mentioned, "Bri, please add that we can only bring in one Whitenmeyer at a time, and Leonard should be first. We don't want to discover that Lyndor has enough energy to wipe all of us out before we remove Leonard. The cousins didn't seem to get along all that well, so I'm pretty sure Lyndor won't share any of his energy with Leonard. Then, of course, everyone else can come at the same time."

Then I added what she shared about calling in the Whitenmeyers, one at a time. "Leonard first, then Lyndor, then the rest of the souls trapped there can come together."

* * *

Kyle

A haggard, monster-ish man appeared in front of Jacob. The man glanced at me and grinned, showing pointy teeth. I assumed this must be Leonard, the doctor of torture.

He held an instrument that looked like an ancient scalpel.

"What the hell are you doing? Get away from him!" Hallelujah, my voice worked.

"Okay, sure. You can take his place." He stepped toward me, whipped the blanket off my body, and suddenly vanished.

"Oh, hell, how'd I get back here?" Jacob stared at me. "You're naked. And why am I naked and stuck on a wall?"

"Leonard was ready to use his scalpel on you. I got his attention, so he came after me and disappeared before he cut into me." My head finally moved like normal, and so did my appendages.

"I think he dropped that scalpel on your cot beside your hand. What do you think he was going to cut?" Jacob chuckled. "I know, it's not funny. I could be toolless, or he could have taken yours."

The thought of that made me cringe. I touched my fingers around and felt the blade. "Dang, I think I cut my finger."

"Just move the tip of your finger on top of it to move the blade enough to reach the handle. You've got this." Jacob studied my every movement. "A little more toward the left, and you should be able to get a good grip."

I clasped the handle and wrapped my fingers around it, maneuvering the blade over the rope-like binding that attached my wrist to the cot. With my hand free, I went to town on my neck binding, wrist, and legs. I climbed off the cot and headed toward Jacob. "What the heck kind of cuffs are binding you to the wall? They look bronze and require a key. Although, I know how to pick a lock." I got to work on the neck brace first, happy to see Jacob's feet safely planted on the ground. It only took a minute or two to open all the cuffs holding him to the wall.

"Okay, where do you think our clothes are?" He walked across the room, checking all surfaces and cupboards.

"Here." I pulled our clothing from a canister on the floor, probably used for trash or laundry. We quickly dressed. I cracked the door and looked out. "I don't see anything ominous. I also don't hear anything. Maybe everyone is sleeping."

I opened the door all the way, walked to the railing, and looked down. The place buzzed with half-dressed or naked women and men. The whole floor seemed to move in a waft of unique rhythms, like an orgy party, not that I'd ever gone to one. I shook my head at Jacob. "I'm unsure how to get us back into our bodies, but we must hide until I do. Leonard vanished so fast, like a fade-out. I think he's probably low on energy. But, I don't know about..."

"Were you about to say, Lyndor?" He looked exactly like the pictures on the internet. "My cousin has gone to his room for now and asked me to check on you." He held an old handgun, pointed at my heart. "I can shoot you both, or you can join the party downstairs. You won't be able to leave the house as you're now part of its history. You'll remain here forever and might as well enjoy yourselves. If not, we do away with you. Only players get to stay."

Lyndor waved to someone from down below, holding up two fingers. Two scantily dressed women walked down the hall to greet us a moment later.

"You could use a nice hot bath and massage." She gently slid her hand down my cheek, continuing downward to the crotch of my pants. "Oh, my, I feel parts of you need attention." She smiled, swept her hand into mine, and pulled me to a room a few doors from where we'd left.

I looked back at Jacob, who was getting the same kind of treatment I did, only heading in the opposite direction. I ended up in a room with a large bed, a clawed bathtub for two, and towels and robes to complete the scene.

"May I undress you? The bath is ready for occupancy." Her warm smile seemed genuine.

"I'd rather talk with you than take a bath. I got kidnapped and brought here without permission, not for sex. Let me add, I am in love and engaged to the woman I plan to marry." I walked to the edge of the bed and sat. "Are you all right with sitting here? I have some questions I'd like to ask?"

She stepped over to the end of the bed, pulled on one of the robes, tied it around her waist, and then sat next to me. "I've never experienced a man that only wanted to talk, especially not one that wanted to ask questions. Why would someone bring you here without your permission?" She tilted her head ever so slightly and reached out her hand. "My name is Anne, by the way."

I shook her hand. "I'm Kyle. My significant other is Bri. Leonard Whitenmeyer took me. Tell me about him."

Her lips pinched together as her brows drew inward. She glanced around the room. "Is this a test? Mr. Whitenmeyer..." Her face paled.

"I know him, sort of. I know he abuses the women here. Does he do surgeries on the women?" I recalled the pictures of the women with enlarged breasts, wondering what else he had changed on them.

"What can you possibly do to save us? He'll have you kidnapping women to bring here sooner or later. That's how he gets new blood. Or sometimes, one of his clients brings a woman along for trade. I was one of those. I thought we were going to Chicago to get married and ended up getting left here. I see my fiancé, now and then, come in with another woman. He leaves her just like he left me. None of the women want to be here. We were all captured, tortured until we submitted to stay, and now get abused by most clients who like fast and rough." She glanced toward the window, looking sad. Tears slid down her cheek. "We can't go

145

outside. The only thing out there are the graves of women with diseases, who got too old, didn't live through the torturing, or died giving birth. There are a lot of baby graves. Occasionally, someone will take a baby, and that baby lives, but none of the birthing mothers know if their baby will die or live."

I couldn't imagine living like that...and who had any idea this place was a death trap for women and babies. I was sure none of the clients had a clue...and I was also sure most loved torturing or abusing the women here. No boundaries. It had a reputation from its clientele. Word of mouth traveled fast back then, especially for a place like this.

She rose from the bed and walked to the window, pulling open the light cotton curtains. "I would rather die and move on toward the light so I can be with the rest of my family." She turned toward me. "Tell me you can help us all get out of here."

What I understood from Anne's statement, she didn't know she'd already died. "I'm pretty sure my Bri and the others involved in your rescue are working hard to find a way to get us out of here...all of us. Keep the faith that will happen. Maybe you can quietly share with the other women here. They all will be with their families soon so they can prepare. Leonard and Lyndor cannot know this. So, if there are snitches among the ladies, don't share with them. We don't want either of those men to get wind of our rescue...or yours."

146

Chapter Fourteen

Kyle

Anne and I left the room to find Jacob. If we got caught by Lyndor or Leonard, we'd pretend to have a private orgy, even though our goal was to find a hideout until we could get rescued. For whatever reason, Leonard wanted to physically hurt Jacob and me, which made me even more curious about what happened to Leonard during his childhood. Bri and I figured Leonard had gotten traumatized by his father taking him in to watch surgeries at such a young age. But what else did his father do to him?

When Anne and I entered their room, Jacob and the woman sat in the claw tub facing each other. Jacob looked up with a blush on his face.

"Whatcha doin'?" I couldn't resist pushing his buttons.

"Janelle, these men will help us escape this nightmare." Anne grabbed the two robes and towels off the bed and carried them to the bathers. "Let's discuss what we can do to help these men."

Janelle nodded and quickly rose from the water, grabbing a towel and a robe.

Jacob took the towel, dried himself, and then got dressed. "Do you have a plan?"

I looked at Anne. "Is Janelle a friend of yours? Do you trust her?"

"With my life." Anne went to Janelle's side, placing her arm around Janelle's waist. "She took me under her wing as soon as my husband-to-be left me here. We're more like sisters."

"I'll do everything I can to save the women in this mansion. I'll help you." Janelle smiled at Anne and nodded toward Jacob.

"There's not much we can do from here except hide until our group figures out how to take Leonard and Lyndor away. By getting them out of here, those left behind should become freed to join their families." I almost added, 'in the light realm.' Those words made me think of Bri as she'd said them during past rituals. I didn't wish to scare these women if Leonard had kept their deaths a secret. "Anne and Janelle, if you could share this information with the women you trust, I'm hoping everyone will help us stay hidden from the Whitenmeyer men until they get removed." Again, I wanted to add, 'the rest of you will gain the ability to move on as the power holding you here will disintegrate.' But I couldn't spook them and lose their trust with something that sounded so crazy.

Anne hugged Janelle. "We're going home, Janelle, and we'll reconnect with our families."

"And with possibly some of the babies I lost to that madman," Janelle added as her water-filled eyes overflowed and rolled down her face.

The door to the room blew open, and Lyndor walked in. "Why are you all dressed? I thought I'd find you in the throes of lust." He barked a chuckle, sounding nothing like a swoon-worthy actor.

Janelle untied her robe and let it drop to the floor, exposing her naked body. "Would you care to join us? We were getting ready for a foursome orgy."

Lyndor smiled. A smoldering expression lit his face as he stared at Jacob. "I'm tempted to try that one." He tilts his head and saunters across the room to stand in front of Jacob, sitting on the bed. "What do you think?" He studied Jacob. Then Lyndor slowly opened the front of his pants and slid them down. The rest of us went mute. "You looked so fit and flavorful hanging naked on the wall." His grin looked vulgar, and the part sticking out of his pants grew hard.

"Men aren't my forte." Jacob moved to the side, away from Lyndor's crotch.

"Have you ever tried a man before?" Lyndor slid in front of Jacob, swaying so his man part danced in Jacob's face.

"Hey, look, man. I don't do men, nor would I ever do a man." Jacob shoved

Lyndor out of the way and grabbed Janelle. His eyes roved over her nakedness, making her blush. "Now, this one, I want." Jacob pulled her to the other side of the bed, leaving Lyndor standing with his pants down on the opposite side.

I waited for Lyndor to attack, but instead, he yanked his pants higher so he could walk to me, leaving the front open so his man part hung out. "What about you? You must want to taste me like I tasted you." His tongue slithered out of his mouth, and my stomach churned.

"You did not taste me, nor would I ever allow that to happen." I wanted to punch him in the crotch and knock him off his feet. "Get away from me."

"Oh, aren't you the tough man. Even though the rest of your body couldn't move spread out on that surgical table, that thing," he pointed at my crotch, "grew to monster size when I..."

I ran toward Lyndor and knocked him down. I raised my foot to stomp on the front of his dumb-ass-opened pants when Leonard slammed through the door and punched me in the ear. I saw stars briefly before I went down like a sack of potatoes. I got back on my feet, realizing what hit my ear was the butt of a pistol. I stared down the beast end of it, now pointed at my head.

"Get the hell against that wall. And you," he swung the gun toward Jacob, who was still under the covers with Janelle, "get over here, or I'll shoot you and the woman." He cocked the gun, and Jacob moved, still fully dressed. Janelle followed Jacob out of bed but then stepped over to Anne, who handed her the robe that Janelle had dropped on the floor. "You women leave, now." Leonard waved them out of the room and then glanced at Lyndor, still sitting on the floor with his pants open. "Put that thing away, or I'll shoot it off."

"You will not do that. You need my money and the women I bring to our business."

"Maybe so, but the next time you come to stay for a while, maybe you should consider bringing a young boy-man that likes to play your sex games." He huffed, sounding disgusted. "I mean it. Put that thing away, or I'll dump hot wax on it." He moved toward a burning candle.

"Oh, that sounds like a great idea, Leo."

Leonard shook his head. "Get your pants up."

Lyndor stood, pushed his outraged appendage back inside the gap, and pulled the front of his pants together. "I'm hungry for sex. It's difficult to watch the girls and guys play with each other downstairs and not receive any satisfaction for myself."

Again, Leonard made a disgusted-sounding bark toward Lyndor. "Now tie their hands behind their back, and then get out and find someone to satisfy you."

152

I noticed that Leonard seemed to fade in and out. The angrier he became, the more often he would pale out. I wondered how he rebuilt his energy level. Maybe we could figure it out between Jacob, Janelle, Anne, and me. The girls must know where and how he gathered his power. Or perhaps they'd never realized his situation...that he was dead. If they didn't recognize that they were all dead, why would they believe Leonard and Lyndor were?

After Lyndor tied our hands, which shocked me as my bindings weren't tight, he headed toward the door. "Are you all right with these guys by yourself?"

"Why would you ask that stupid question in front of them, especially when I'm holding a gun toward them." Leonard focused on Lyndor even though the gun remained pointed at us.

"Well, for one thing, yesterday, you didn't have any ammunition. I wanted to make sure you do now."

I watched Leonard's face turn blood red. If steam could have shot out of his ears, it would have at that moment.

Leonard turned his attention to us. "Turn around and face the wall."

"You aren't going to shoot them in this room, are you?" Lyndor stood at the open door.

"If you don't get out of here, I'm going to blow your head off," Leonard yelled.

Jacob looked at me and whispered, "It's been great getting to know you, Kyle. I'm glad to have met everyone at SPI."

I could tell that Jacob thought this was our last living moment, but I knew differently. There's no way Leonard could kill our souls. If anything, getting shot should send us back into our bodies and out of this realm. *Although, I never did understand the soul part of us completely.*

"I'm a watcher." Leonard moved closer, and I felt the business end of the pistol against my back. "I want to watch you with one or two of my girls. After you had your fun, I want to watch this guy." The pistol barrel moved off my back, and I figured it now pressed Jacob's. "I like it fast and furious, slapping breasts, twisting nipples, and slamming home in the front or back." He laughed like a madman while adding more horrifying graphic details.

I turned my head enough to see his face. His tongue slithered out like a snake's forked tongue, making me want to puke. He saw me looking and cracked my head against the wall.

"Keep that head turned, or I'll bring Lyndor back up here so he can have his way with you." He plastered his body against the back of mine, pressing me harder into the wall.

What in the hell was this brothel about? I couldn't believe how out of control this freak became. And then another thought came to mind. *Make him angry and keep him weak so the rescue can happen.* I raised my foot and shot it behind me, crunching it into Leonard's knee. He went down. I turned and kicked him in the face as Jacob kicked the pistol from his hand.

Blood ran from the corner of his mouth as he spat out, "You better hope to hell I don't see your woman again because the next time, I'll make her mine forever and then cut her in all the right places. I covered her with burns the last time, especially on her most tender areas."

Now, that scared me. I was afraid not only for Bri but I'd also blown a fuse of his anger. I didn't count on Leonard using Bri against me, and Bri never shared everything that sick-minded monster had done to her. I stomped on his face again, knocking him out, and then his body faded out of sight.

Between Jacob and me, we freed each other. I think that might have been Lyndor's intention for leaving our bindings so loose. I picked up the pistol and found it empty of ammo, so I hid it under the mattress.

"Let's go find Anne and Janelle. I'm fairly certain Lyndor will have other activities keeping him busy." I chuckled.

"Did you see the size of his..."

Before Jacob finished, I waved my hand and answered, "Yes, and honestly, it terrified me."

We left the room and peeked over the rail. The sounds and smells of the orgy below wafted through the air. I'd never seen so many naked bodies at such crazy angles. Also, numerous groups of more than two were engaged with each other, some roughly. Jacob pointed to the corner.

"Oh, my gods, have you ever seen that done?" Two women and a man enjoyed different angles with each other. "I've got such a hard-on right now."

I couldn't believe how bound up I became from watching the romp on the main floor, as it actually sickened me. I had difficulty visually combing the floor, wondering if aphrodisiacs had gone airborne. My breath rasped out of me. "We need to find Anne and Janelle. Do you see them?"

"No, but look at the bottom of the stairway." Lyndor found a man and a woman in the throes of lust and took on the challenge of the male. "Can you believe the balls Lyndor has? I can't believe that guy didn't knock Lyndor on his ass and then beat the crap out of him."

"Well, I think these guys are doing some drugs. Did they have weed back in the 1800s?" I gave one last glance around the room for Janelle and Anne. "I don't see the women downstairs. Let's look in some of these rooms." I walked over to the first door and opened it to get a look. A couple went at it on the bed and another couple in the tub, but neither of the women was Anne or Janelle.

We went down the rooms of the whole third floor except for Leonard's—the last door at the end of the hall. We found every space occupied by one or more couples, but none contained our girls. We headed down one flight to the second floor and reached the fourth door, where we found them. The girls were alone, sitting in the room, wearing robes, and drinking tea. Both looked up at the same time.

Anne jumped to her feet. "Kyle, Jacob, are either of you hurt?" She touched my ear, making me wince. "This looks nasty, a little blood and swelling. You'll have a bruise. Can you hear all right?"

Janelle walked over to Jacob, checking him over. "Are you okay?"

"We are both doing all right, other than getting a birds-eye-view of what's happening on the main floor. I had no idea of all the different ways a person can have..." Jacob's eyes widened, and he shut his mouth. Then he pulled Janelle into his arms for a quick hug. "We thought we lost you, ladies. Glad you're both okay."

"Sit with us and have some tea. Perhaps we can discuss how we'll enforce your plan?" Anne poured two more cups of tea and set them on a table for four. "Come and sit with us."

"How many women live and work here?" I asked, sitting between Anne and Janelle. Jacob sat across from me.

"There are twenty pleasure-working women, five housekeeping women, and four cooks—two men and two women. Six to eight men also stay in a lodge on the other side of the woods. They grow gardens and protect the property for us. Once a week, they get free favors from one of the pleasure workers as part of their wage." Anne looked at Janelle. "Did I include everyone?"

Janelle added, "Two older women act as nurses for any required healing or surgeries. Leonard performs surgeries for most new girls, and a nurse became necessary for the patient's recovery. Leonard only does the surgery but doesn't involve himself with the patient's recovery. He's created a couple of monsters from his sordid surgeries. If he isn't happy with the outcome, we believe he puts the patient down, like a farmer puts down a sick animal." Janelle sucked in a breath. "I've lost several friends from his surgeries."

"You are one of the lucky ones, Janelle. You came with a perfect body." Anne smiled, reaching across the small table to pat Janelle's hand.

Suddenly, soft music played right below the room, slow dancing kind of music.

"Janelle, would you dance with me?" Jacob stood from his chair and grasped one of Janelle's hands. "I would be honored." He bowed.

I grinned at Jacob, realizing he had a thing for Janelle. It struck my heart like a stab, knowing it couldn't last. I thought a lot about Bri at that moment, not only for the solid love I felt for her but also for the hope that the team made progress on how we would get rescued before Leonard got his mojo back.

Chapter Fifteen

Kyle

The last thing I recalled about the night before was Jacob and Janelle dancing for hours, and Anne had shared some of her worst experiences with the clientele until I fell asleep on the bed.

Anne lay beside me, still dressed in her robe, and I had remained entirely clothed. The sun crept through the trees and in between the curtains. I quietly climbed out of bed, noticing that Jacob and Janelle hadn't slept in this room. I walked to the window and looked out. The snowstorm had stopped, but had it quit in the earth realm? I wandered out the door to see what I could over the rail. Naked bodies lay everywhere, in every pose possible, and some were still in the throes of lust, reminding me how much I missed Bri.

Not sure all the sex scenes I'd witnessed here would ever leave my memory as I glanced at the corner where Jacob and I saw the two girls and a guy. They lay together, intertwined and asleep on the floor. The guy and gal at the bottom of the steps with Lyndor from last night were gone. I looked around a bit longer for Lyndor and saw him with another man. Guess he got his satisfaction.

The door behind me creaked, and I turned to look. Anne stepped out dressed and ready for the day.

"How are you feeling today?" She glanced down at the display of naked bodies. "They will continue enjoying each other all day, taking breaks for a bath or meal, but always going back to the main floor for more. Leonard puts an aphrodisiac into the water or other drinks to ensure everyone is sated. Some people lose track of time and stay here for days. No one leaves complaining." She smiled. "Did you want to join that group?"

"No, never. I've already told you about Bri, the love of my life, who is also my only intimate partner." I thought about all that Leonard must have done to Bri while she had gotten held captive here. I wondered if Lyndor had taken advantage whenever Leonard left her in a room alone. Pictures shuffled through my head and became unsettling. I stared at Anne. "Do you know my Bri? She's been here a couple of times."

"Yes, I met her. She's beautiful, with those brilliant, midnight blue eyes and full lips. Did she share what happened while Leonard and Lyndor had her?" Anne stepped away from the rail. "Perhaps we should go back into the room in case Leonard starts making his rounds. We never want to anger him."

"Oh, I'm beginning to think we should always anger him. That's what seems to make him disappear. He uses so much energy when full of rage that it weakens his power supply. I suggest you pass that on to everyone. Instead of treading lightly not to piss him off, stomp around. Make his anger grow until he vanishes. It's the only way my team from back home can get control of Leonard and Lyndor." I followed Anne back into the room and closed the door. "Isn't there a lock on any of these doors?"

"No, only Leonard has a lock on his room door." Anne pulled out a chair for me but remained standing. "I'm going downstairs to get some food and drinks. I want to check on Janelle, also. I can send Jacob down here if he's awake. Would you want me to?"

"If Jacob's awake, tell him to come to your room. We can talk about a few things."

Anne stopped at the door. "I want you to know Bri is a strong woman. She never faltered during anything Leonard did to her. And Lyndor, he's a pussycat at heart. Although he acts interested in Bri, that only angers his cousin. As you've seen, Lyndor's biggest interest is in men, not women."

Before Anne walked out the door, I asked, "Did you keep watch over her?"

"No one knew that, but yes. I wanted to make sure Bri had plenty of water and food or if she needed a poultice for healing any wounds that Leonard had inflicted. Most of the time, Bri slept through my visits to her...even when she drank water, her eyes rarely opened. I think Leonard must have drugged her."

"What kind of drugs would he use?" I stood and stepped closer to Anne.

"Maybe opium? I know he injects something into his patients that numbs their bodies and closes off their voices. They can't move or talk."

I couldn't even guess what that would be, but I knew he'd done that to me and Jacob. "Thanks, Anne. Especially for helping Bri out while she was here. That means a lot."

Anne reached up and patted my cheek. "I see why you love her. She's a strong, beautiful woman that reminds me of my younger sister, who I haven't seen in years."

Anne had no idea of how many years had passed.

"What year were you born?"

"1862."

"What year is it now?" I added out of curiosity.

She looked at me as if I'd lost my mind. "Well, it's 1887."

"What year were you left here?"

"I don't understand why you ask these questions, as they crush my heart." She took a deep breath and sighed. "Albert left me here in 1877."

My mouth dropped open. Anne had been only fifteen, so had lived here for ten years. I grabbed her and gave her a big hug, stepping back afterward. "I'm so sorry Albert robbed you of your youth. Tell me Leonard did not do surgery on you."

"Oh, he wanted to, but Janelle stopped him. I believe he'd fallen in love with Janelle, even though they never had intimacy. He never had intimacy with anyone, only watched others having it. I think Janelle is still his favorite. She gets away with a lot. Maybe she knows a secret about him that the rest don't and uses it against him." Anne had pulled the curtains open, and her eyes glittered from the sunlight streaming through the window. "I've often wondered that because their relationship seemed so odd, even to this day."

"Anne, because you and Janelle are so close, you should ask her if she's ever seen Leonard naked." I had a feeling Leonard might have some defect with his genitals, which made me question his father. I wondered if Leonard's father used his son as a guinea pig for some surgeries.

"Why..." Suddenly her brows rose, and her mouth dropped open. "Oh, heavens. That makes so much sense. He doesn't have intimacy because he can't...and why can't he?" Her eyes settled on mine. "Do you think there's something wrong with him?"

A hardy laugh blew out of my mouth before I could stop it, and then I couldn't reel it in for a moment.

"There isn't anything funny about that, and honestly, that explains why he acts as he does. Oh, my goodness. That poor man."

"Anne, ask Janelle but don't go on about it. She can't think we've been talking about Leonard's body, and she will if you already know everything. You need to look and act surprised with whatever she shares."

Anne nodded, walked out the door, and quietly closed it.

Our conversation gave me a lot to think about, and if what I believed happened to Leonard, it was amazing he wasn't a serial killer. Well, he did murder many women and babies, so in truth, he was a killer. *I wonder if Bri ever put this scenario together.*

When we investigated the grounds, we would require KPD Officer Morrison's cadaver dog, Buster.

* * *

It felt like I'd stared out the window at the mansion grounds for hours, imagining all the area Buster would need to cover when someone rapped on the door. I hurried over and opened it.

Jacob stood there with pink cheeks and a smirk on his face.

"What's going on?" I pulled him into the room and shut the door.

"I've never met anyone like Janelle. I've fallen hard for her." He pushed my shoulder.

"What the hell am I going to do when we leave? Can I take her with us?"

I shook my head. "Why would you go and do something like fall for a ghost? What were you thinking? Plus, you know we are now in the year 1887." I led him to a chair as his face went pale.

"Are you kidding me? I had no idea about the year. Why didn't I know we were going back in time?"

I tipped my head back, giving myself a minute to calm down before I went too far by belittling him. I studied him for another second.

Jacob's whole body slumped, his eyes closed as his head dropped forward.

"Jacob, you're the one that called SPI about something going on outside this mansion. You thought women were in trouble there, and then it went to a possible cult of women, but we figured out they were ghosts attached to the mansion...the ancient, dilapidated building surrounded by an old overgrown forest. Get up and look out the window."

I helped him out of the chair and led him to the window.

"Oh, my, Gods! I don't know why I didn't connect the dots. The date is over a century ago. Right now, I think Janelle feels the same about me as I feel about her. I can't get enough of her. What have I done? Does she know we're from the future?"

"I'm pretty sure they don't realize we're from the future, although our clothing differs from theirs. During their timeline, Janelle and Anne have been locked in here for at least ten years. Maybe it would help to know that Janelle is also Leonard's number one favorite. We think she might know something about Leonard that no one else knows, not even his cousin."

Jacob's jaw tensed. "Please tell me she isn't in love with Leonard."

"I don't know why she would be...but I believe there is some relationship between those two that isn't like anyone else's, according to Anne." Just as I said her name, Anne walked in with her hands full of food or drinks, followed by Janelle, who also had her hands overflowing.

Jacob and I both jumped up and hurried over to relieve the women of their load. They only shared a little as everything was stacked awkwardly in their arms. They carefully set most of it on the table.

I glanced at Anne for a signal that she'd learned something. I received a nod and wink. So, Leonard had an issue that only Janelle had known, and now, Anne caught wind of it. *When the monster learns we're all aware of his problem; he will create consequences and hellacious havoc.*

"Let's eat. I'm starving." Jacob dug in, flipping mini sandwiches and pastries onto his plate. Janelle set a cup of tea next to his silverware and another by hers.

Anne poured tea for her and me. "We can all help ourselves."

We settled into eating, and the room became so quiet I could hear the others chewing or drinking. "Does anyone have anything they want to talk about?"

Jacob set his fork beside his plate. He turned his head to stare at me. "I want to marry Janelle."

Food sprayed from Janelle's mouth into my face as she sat across the table. With her coughing and choking, I thought she might pass out. Anne slipped out of her chair and pulled Janelle to the floor, making her drop to all four (knees and hands). Then Anne smacked Janelle's back until the choking subsided.

Jacob had gone to all four beside Janelle, attempting to soothe her by talking and rubbing her arm.

Anne stepped away, moving to eat on the bed, and set her drink on the nightstand. I followed her and sat beside her. We stared out the window, trying not to listen to Janelle and Jacob's conversation. They sat on the floor. We couldn't see them from where we sat on the edge of the bed.

I whispered to Anne, "Maybe we should go to Janelle's room and leave them alone here for a while."

"Good idea." We both climbed off the bed, setting our plates and cups on the table.

Jacob and Janelle snuggled in the opposite corner of the room from where Anne and I had sat on the bed.

"Where are you sneaking off to?" Jacob looked up at me. "We can leave, and you can stay here. We've got some business to attend to anyway." He smiled at Janelle and kissed her forehead.

They stood up, brushed themselves off, and hightailed out of there. I could feel the fire burning in Jacob toward Janelle. Then I wondered if she might be an ancestor to a female in our timeline who might be the same age as Jacob. *What were the chances?*

Anne wandered back to the window. "We aren't allowed on the grounds much, so it seems everyone likes looking out their window. I see all kinds of wildlife, like turkeys, coyotes, deer, eagles, raccoons, squirrels, and occasionally, I have seen bobcats. We keep tabs on what we've seen weekly, and the person who sees the most wins. Not that the winner collects anything, but they receive a lot of accolades from everyone else."

"It's great to hear you can enjoy the outdoors, even if you're not out there. But mostly, it's nice that the people here are like one big family, even if no one is thrilled because they miss their family." I walked back to the bed and sat next to Anne. "So, tell me what you learned regarding Leonard."

She turned to face me. "Leonard told Janelle that when he was eight years old, his father had removed his penis and attempted to create a vagina. After five surgeries, Leonard ended up without a penis or a vagina but still had his testicles. That's why he's never had intimacy but likes to watch others having it. During his surgeries, his mother also went missing and never returned. I can't imagine what that must feel like for him."

Chapter Sixteen

Kyle

We never did see Leonard, nor did we hear from Lyndor during the day. I lay in bed alone with my eyes open. A pleasure worker had called Anne away a while ago, and it sounded like Anne wouldn't return to the room. I was not too fond of the feeling that spread through me for these women—the fact they were sex workers and didn't know anything else in their lifetime. They never earned money, only popularity, and what kind of fame would any woman want from this type of popularity? Depending on the men who used and abused them, it could turn out brutal, even deadly. Even though I knew little about her life, I would want to defend her honor if Anne was misused. She reminded me of Bri in ways I didn't realize. Anne's demeanor and personality came across as courageous, and her beauty inside and out would take any man's breath away. Her long blonde hair, fair-skinned, bright green eyes, and slender form reminded me of some of the superstars of my timeline.

Anne and her life impacted me even more toward the love and protective way I felt for Bri. It made me wish that we could save these women...but I guess our end game would send them to the light realm, home to their loved ones. I kept rethinking the whole scenario to wrap my brain around it. I knew similar thoughts were also in Jacob's mind for Janelle. Nothing we did for them now would work toward what had already happened. Everybody here was dead and gone...these were all ghosts from over a hundred years ago...way, way before our time.

* * *

A sound like a gunshot woke me. I sat straight up, realizing the sun had already risen for a new day, so I rushed out of bed. Running through the hallway outside the room drew me to the door, so I cracked it open. Everyone appeared dressed, although their expressions looked pinched and tense, definitely in fear.

I stepped into the hall and stopped the next woman. "What's happened?"

She stared at me sheepishly and shook her head. "Someone just got shot downstairs. I don't know who or if that person is injured or dead. But we must get downstairs fast before Leonard comes looking for us. No telling how many will lose their lives today."

I didn't understand why Leonard would make people feel they had to hurry or get shot. All the workers stayed inside all day, every day. Why would Leonard put unnecessary fear in them if everyone followed the rules, which seemed like what everyone did—unless one of their clients decided to off someone over an anger issue?

What if Leonard found Jacob with Janelle?

"Oh, no." My thoughts went wild. What if Jacob attempted to stop Leonard from taking Janelle away?

Just then, I saw Anne running up the stairway and then toward me. It seemed everyone came running back up the stairs to the second or third floor, most likely afraid for their lives.

I met Anne halfway. "I heard a gunshot," I said.

"I'm so sorry, Kyle." Tears rolled down Anne's cheeks. "Leonard forced everyone to leave the dining room except Janelle and Jacob. I hadn't made it to the door when Leonard shot Jacob."

"What provoked Leonard?" I couldn't believe Jacob would go where Leonard might find him.

"When Leonard entered the room, Jacob was kissing Janelle in the corner." Anne whimpered, closing her eyes, and then leaned into my body. I slid my arm around her to stop her from falling to the floor. Her tears penetrated my shirt as she sobbed. "I don't think Jacob died." As soon as the words left her mouth, another shot sounded.

"I need to see what's happening." I shuffled us up the remaining steps, crossed the floor to our room, and helped her to the bed. "You must be exhausted from your long night. Rest, Anne. Please."

"No, Kyle, you can't go down there. Leonard will shoot you. He asked where you were." Her lips trembled, and her hands shook as she reached for me. "Please, stay." She climbed off the bed and stood beside me. "I'll go check and see what just happened down there. Leonard would expect me to check on Janelle."

Leonard had to deplete his energy, and getting him angry seemed to work best. I had a feeling if I walked into that room now, he would shoot me without hesitation. But maybe I could blindside him by talking about his father. That ought to tip the scales of his anger to a massacre level. Plus, I needed to check on Jacob and make sure that Leonard wouldn't shoot anyone else today, especially Anne or Janelle.

"I'm going down. You stay, so no one else gets shot today." I guided her back to the bed.

She grabbed my hand. "You need to be prepared, Kyle. He will shoot you and throw you and Jacob into a grave."

Little did Anne know if Leonard killed us, Jacob and I wouldn't leave a body behind.

The double door to the dining room stood open. I slowly moved toward it, listening for Leonard or Janelle, but I heard neither. The main floor was empty of people and put back together as if nothing had ever happened over the weekend. The clients must have left before I woke up. I peeked around the doorway and saw no one in the dining room. Then I entered, checking walls and floors for blood splatter, and found no sign of foul play. I moved through the dining room into the kitchen. The two housekeepers stacking dishes looked up at me.

"Did you miss your ride home, sir?" asked the dark-haired woman.

"No. I was looking for a man and a woman." I described both, and the two women looked at each other as if they knew who I had meant. "Would you be so kind as to point me in the right direction to find them?"

Again, the two looked at each other, and finally, the gray-haired woman said, "I don't know about the man you describe, but the woman went with Leonard to his room at the end of the hall on the third floor. And as upset as Leonard acted, I wouldn't disturb them if I were you."

"I heard two gunshots a short time ago. Do you know anything about those?" I watched as they did the same thing staring at each other. "Just tell me the truth. I'm not going to snitch on either of you."

The gray-haired woman rolled her eyes at the other woman and said, "We saw a man drop to the floor from the first shot, and then Leonard walked over and shot him again. The dead man disappeared right before our eyes. I can't tell you how that happened, but the man you described is now gone."

"Thanks. I appreciate your honesty." I left them and headed to the third floor.

Anne waited on the second-floor landing. "Did you see Leonard and Janelle?"

"I'm on my way to see them. The two shots were at Jacob, and we lost him." I felt relieved he'd vanished and sure that he had returned to the team in our timeline. He would tell the group how to knock down Leonard's power, and Lyndor would easily follow wherever Leonard went. Those two seemed attached in a yin/yang sort of way.

Anne studied my face. "You're not upset about the loss of your friend?"

I closed my eyes. Damn, my acting sucked. I took a deep breath and squeezed my eyelids harder, realizing that didn't help the development of a tear. A sigh whipped out before I could stop it. I turned my head away from Anne, unable to explain about Jacob and me—who we were, where we came from, or why we had arrived. "You head back to the room. I'll meet you there in a couple of minutes." Then I hurried up the stairs to the third floor.

* * *

Bri

"Oh, my gosh, I just saw Jacob move." I rushed over to him from sitting on the floor in front of where Kyle lay on the couch. "Jacob, it's Bri." I gently shook him.

Lucky had followed me. "Allow him to awaken on his own. It may take him a few minutes to align himself with the here and now." Grams' voice came through Lucky loud and clear, like always.

I grasped Jacob's hand to ground him as his eyes fluttered open. I waited until he got focused.

He sucked in a deep breath, almost like he'd gotten deprived of oxygen. "I'm back. Oh, my, Gods, I'm really back. Kyle told me if, somehow, we got killed, we would immediately snap back into our bodies and our place in time. Part of me didn't believe him, but...I like that it's true." He gripped my hand harder while he pulled himself into a sitting position. "Thanks for watching over us, Bri. I'm sure everyone is worried. We've been gone for days."

"Well, in this timeline, it's only been hours, but I've been there and done that timeline, so I understand." I glanced over to Kyle, noticing no movement. "Was Kyle with you?"

"Not when Leonard shot me." Jacob lowered his focus toward the floor for a moment. "Honestly, I'm not sure where he was right then. Anne was in the dining room without him."

I didn't understand what that meant but would find out about Anne directly from Kyle later. Still, an extra beat in my heart stopped me for a second, but after a nurturing breath, I knew not to go there.

As if Jacob realized what his words indicated, his eyes widened. "Wow. Anne is not an issue with Kyle. I mean, Anne and Kyle are only good friends. Oh, Gods, I meant to say Kyle talked about you constantly, with me, Anne, and Janelle. It's like you two were already married." He rolled his eyes. "There's no chance that man would feel for anyone as he feels for you, Bri. Even if the woman in question is a ghost." Then he turned solemn, pressing his lips closed for a few seconds. "Except for Janelle, who also is a ghost, and I fell in love with her. I was with her when Leonard shot me. I think he shot me because I was with her."

"That's a lot of information. Did you walk around free? I thought the way you all left, simultaneously with Leonard that he had captured you." I couldn't believe the guys hadn't gotten restrained right away.

"Let Jacob continue, Bri. It seems he has much to share, and we need to hear all of it." Grams' calm voice went to Jacob and me as I watched Jacob glance down at Lucky.

"Thanks, Grams. I'm glad to know you're back unscathed." Jacob smiled at Lucky and bent down to pat his head. "Well, we were captured. I woke up hanging on a wall, and Kyle had gotten strapped to a cot that looked like an ancient surgical table. I don't want to go into graphics," he glances toward Lucky, "but we were both naked. Leonard was about to do surgery on your significant other, and maybe me." He explained Lyndor and Leonard, the big scene in the surgery room, how Leonard lost his power, fading in and out until he vanished, and then Kyle and Jacob escaped to hide.

I texted the rest of the team, who were doing last-minute stuff in the pole barn for the upcoming ritual at midnight: *'Jacob woke up and is filling us in on what happened while in the spirit realm. Grams and I think you should hear his information before the ritual. Please hurry inside.'* I looked at the clock, realizing that it would happen in a few hours, at midnight.

Chapter Seventeen

Kyle

I hurried down the third-story hall and stopped at the door Bri couldn't open when we first visited this dilapidated mansion in our timeline. The doorknob looked like a newer, shinier version of the antique ornamental one we saw. Our hearing had gone out back then from whatever was behind this door. She mentioned a horrid stench also. I recalled the utter terror in Bri's eyes when she told me to run. And we'd broken some of the steps running out of the mansion to the SUV.

Now, I leaned my ear against the same wooden arched door in time to hear Janelle scream, sounding out of control. I lifted my leg at the ready to kick it in when Leonard hollered, "He's not dead. Stop screaming."

Moving back into a listening-at-the-door mode, I heard their conversation.

"What are you talking about? Jacob's not dead. I watched you shoot him twice!" It sounded like Janelle ran across the room, perhaps toward Leonard. She screeched like a banshee.

Then the sound of a slap. "Pull yourself together. I can explain everything if you give me a few minutes to figure out how. It won't make sense to you as everyone here is already dead. You're all caught in a loop. Jacob and Kyle came from the future. They know how to break through the spirit realm, and I believe they can do it because of a woman named Bri."

"You sound like a lunatic. Did you bump your head? Did you take any of your surgical medications?" Janelle ran toward the door, so I moved out of the way in case she opened it. "Let me out, now!"

"I'm not letting you leave until you understand what I tell you. I've been protecting all of you for over a hundred years. Without me, all of this will go away. Do you want that?"

I realized Leonard had become a traumatized child, and his demented thinking had turned psychopathic and sociopathic.

"You have lost your mind, Leonard. I can understand the trauma you've grown up with from your father, but now, you're telling me we're all dead? If we're dead, what are we? Ghosts?" Janelle laughed until it turned into something more like hysteria. The doorknob rattled, but the door didn't budge. When she finally caught her breath, she added, "I'm leaving. I should have run away from here a long time ago."

"If you leave the grounds, you'll never rest in peace." Leonard moved toward the door. "I won't allow you to leave, Janelle.

You're the closest thing I have to a family. You know me, understand what I've been through, and have stayed by my side all these years. Why do you want to leave now? You will never see that man again. In fact, the other man, Kyle, will pay the ultimate sacrifice for coming here and breaking apart all I've protected. This mansion, everyone living here, and these grounds are mine, and no one will take it from me."

"Open the door, Leonard. I will kill myself if you leave me in this room."

"But you're already dead, my dear Janelle."

I heard struggling, slapping, things falling or being thrown, and breaking glass.

Then Leonard said, "I truly hoped it wouldn't come to this."

"What are you doing?"

"I'm gagging and tying you."

"No! What's in the syringe?"

"Something that will take your anger away and relax you."

Janelle no longer talked.

I stood there at a loss for what to do. It's not like I could change their history. They were already dead, on a repeating loop of their past. That wouldn't change. How could I save either of them in my spirit form anyway? I needed to get back, and Bri had never prepared me for how my soul returned to my body. Maybe she didn't know. Right now, I needed to move away from this door and figure out how to enrage Leonard so much that his energy became depleted.

I hurried down the hall and took the steps to the second floor. I might be safe in Anne's room because Leonard hadn't seen us together. I tapped on the door and then opened it. No Anne. An eerie feeling stabbed through my chest. I had no idea what part of Leonard's loop we were in now, but eeriness had filled me with desperation. I hoped the team hadn't already attempted the ritual, because it failed if they did. That should have happened days ago.

Suddenly, a bellowing voice rattled the entire mansion as if every wall had a speaker turned up one hundred percent. "I'm going to find you, Kyle, and when I do, you'll feel the wrath of suffering. The kind I've felt for years. You'll be lost to your Bri because you'll be mine."

Even the floor shook under my feet, so much I fell, lying on my backside. Then I remembered Bri said that time went much faster here than in our timeline. Was it hours per one hour or days per so many hours? Maybe they hadn't performed the ritual yet. I needed to act fast because Leonard's energy had returned to full force.

* * *

Bri

183

All of us had gathered in the pole barn, ready to start in twenty minutes. I'd gone over the ritual first with Grams, the group and I practiced a couple of times on the required mantra, and all the gear and extra possible essentials were set into place. Our plan seemed solid, and we prepared for success.

Jacob tapped my shoulder. "We'll get Kyle back, right? I know our main theme here is to take out Leonard and Lyndor and save all the people they've enslaved, but that also includes Kyle, right?"

His words stilled me, leaving me without a breath to spare. Thankfully, Lucky stood right beside me, so Grams responded through him, "Jacob, you know Kyle wants to return. With his determination and ours, his spirit will reenter his body. He'll come safely back."

Jacob looked at me. "You believe he'll come safely back?"

"Of course I do. You did. So did Grams, and so did I...several times. Kyle will also."

* * *

Kyle

My whole body vibrated like I might explode, and Leonard appeared, standing beside me with a different gun.

"Go ahead and shoot me, you old geezer. I'll disappear, and you won't have to see me

184

again." I attempted to stand, but that crazy madman shot me in the leg. "You missed my kill spot." I cringed, feeling every sense of the pain, but determination got me back up, standing.

Then he laughed like an insane psycho. "Oh, no." He laughed harder, drilling my brain with stabs of pressure that made me want to scream. "I just had to lame you so you can't knock me down. Now, I can move you after I put your lights out." One second later, he kicked my good leg and pinned me under his weight. Then he stabbed a needle into me, filling my arm with only Gods-know-what.

"What did you just give me?" My breathing changed immediately, and my vision quickly turned for the worse. The room spun, and a curtain of darkness covered me into oblivion. "I'm gonna..." The rest of my words left me, as did all feelings and sensitivities, like floating in nothing with pitch black surrounding me.

* * *

When I came awake and attempted to open my eyes, the bright light made me close them. I wondered if I had died and gone into the light instead of back to where my human body lay at James and Sandy's. When I tried to sit up, I realized my body was bound to a surgical table like before, which made me uneasy, like a sacrificial lamb. I could guess what Leonard had in mind for me. If he couldn't have Bri, neither could I. He would make sure of it by doing to me what his father had done to him.

"Well, so you've joined me for the surgery. Good boy."

"I'm not your boy."

He ignored my comment and continued, "I'll give you a play-by-play of what I remove, or would you rather be surprised by it when I've finished? Up to you." He chuckled, and I wanted so badly to punch his face.

"I have to wonder did your father do what he did to you so that you wouldn't procreate? What kind of a child were you, anyway? Were you nicer to your mother, or did your father get her out of the picture before your surgeries?"

"What do you know of my surgeries?"

I still couldn't see him due to that dang light, but I could tell my words raised his anger by the nasty pitch in his voice. So, I decided to get right to the point. "I know you can't get your rocks off because you have no penis." The words, descriptive and mean-as-hell, flew out of my mouth to send him into a rage. The more his temper raised, the lower his energy level, and with no power, the team could direct him to where he needed to go.

But Leonard had remained in the room and said, "We'll see about that. I will remove yours and have Janelle sew it on me. We've been waiting for someone like you, who could cross spiritual boundaries and still be alive on the other side. That means your spirit body might work. None of the men in the loop worked out. The appendage always found its way back to its original owner."

I had a hard time believing what I was hearing. Janelle wouldn't do that for him. Not now, after he shot and killed Jacob. Or would she? I honestly didn't know much about Janelle. Maybe she was a freak just like Leonard; perhaps they knew I stood outside their door listening. They'd had a long time living this loop, and Leonard would need someone trained to perform surgeries like he did, at least a nurse. "Janelle would never do that. She's too honorable a woman."

Then I heard a shuffle and a female giggle. "I'm afraid you've got me all wrong, Kyle. We would have used Jacob, but Leonard got jealous and took him out of the picture. Then he decided he could use your part, and he's positive Bri will show up looking for you. Instead of finding you, he can perform for her."

That didn't sound safe or possible.

Then Janelle and Leonard laughed, probably because I went silent. To them, everything we'd talked about must have sounded hilarious. "Okay, may we share what's actually going to happen with him, Leonard?" A few more chuckles escaped Janelle.

"Of course, dear."

"Well, Jacob shared what was going to happen in your timeline. A ritual would call Leonard and Lyndor, and all of us who live in this house, so some of us will go to mother earth for clean-up, and some may automatically go into the light realm. Leonard will take a detour and end up inside your body, and your imprisoned spirit will never escape. For me, I've always wanted to visit mother earth. I'm ready for a new adventure."

I wished I could see her face to know if she told the truth...if either of them said it. Either story left me out of Bri's life.

"You both make me sick with your ridiculous stories." I couldn't move to fight my restraints, and I couldn't even shift my weight to knock over the table for a little delay in the surgery. I took a deep breath and kept my eyes closed as I sent a mental message to Grams and Bri. "Start the ritual now." *And then wondered, will they receive it in time?*

Chapter Eighteen

Bri

"Bri, do you feel a calling sensation?" Lucky snuggled close to my leg as Grams spoke through him.

"I sense something is wrong, and we must start the ritual," I told Grams. "Everyone move to your position, make sure the smoky crystal on the floor is directly in front of you, and light your tapers." We'd already smudged each other and the room with white sage. Everyone had a sea-salt spray water bottle located on the floor beside them. "Everybody has protection stones around your neck or inside your pocket, correct? We need to start now."

Everyone lit their candle and stood at the ready. I stood on the outer side of our sea salt and lavender circle with Lucky beside me. To my left stood James and then Max. To my right stood Sandy and Luke, and then Jacob stood across from me. Everyone's eyes leveled on me.

"Everyone, please touch your heart with your left hand, and repeat after me: 'I am filled with love and light; the Divine is my shield.'" We repeated it three times. I nodded my head, the signal I would start the ritual.

"Mother Earth, Come Now." A shimmer of green light wisped between Sandy and me. Lucky moved to the opposite side of me. She shimmered into a beautiful young woman dressed in plants and colorful moss, with flower blossoms for hair and tree branches for arms and legs. She nodded to me, Lucky, and Jacob, already knowing we were the only ones who could see her. "Thank you for joining us," I said, and the others responded with the exact words.

"Guardian Angels of everyone in this group, Come Now." The team repeated my words. Each person stood tall, glancing around to see their angels, possibly. "Thank you for your presence, protection, wisdom, and guidance." Everybody repeated what I said.

I could tell James felt his angels around him. And Grams and I watched ours shimmer into sight, along with Lucky's. Our personal Guardian Angels surrounded each of us. Jacob wore a giant smile as he glanced around, seeing several angels at his sides and behind him. Everyone seemed to have a fair count of shimmery light beings. Even though they couldn't see or feel their presence, they responded as if they did.

I nodded to everyone. "Please, prepare for our next guest." Everyone nodded in return.

"Guardian Angels of Leonard Whitenmeyer, Come Now." Shimmering light went directly to the center of the circle and broke apart into bodies of light as if they knew where to locate and what to do. "Thank you for your presence, protection, wisdom, and guidance."

"Leonard Whitenmeyer, Come Now." All of the angels and our team repeated the words two more times.

The stench of rotten eggs arrived and filled the room, announcing an angry spirit had arrived. "Everyone, remain calm." The odor smelled the same as what I recalled when Kyle and I entered the mansion to investigate that first time. But I didn't see Leonard's spirit now.

"He isn't here," Jacob stated.

Grams said, "Give him a minute. I feel he doesn't have enough energy to make his appearance." A moment later, Grams added, "I think Kyle's body needs to come in here, just in case Leonard's spirit went to Kyle instead."

One of Leonard's Guardians stepped toward me. "You must bring your friend in here after you've prepared him. He requires protection."

"But he's unconscious, and we didn't smudge him. Grams, what are your thoughts?"

"I think the men should bring Kyle's body in here after you've successfully prepped him for a possible assault.

Leonard's angel sounds like there is a plan in motion right now. Bri, call in Kyle's Guardian Angels."

I quickly stepped back in place and said, "Guardian Angels of Kyle Benton, Come Now. Thank you for your presence, protection, wisdom, and guidance." I glanced around the circle at our team. "Now, run, guys. Your angels will surround and protect you. Bring Kyle back."

Sandy bent down and picked up the sage smudge stick off the floor she'd used for us earlier. "Here, James. Take this with you. You know what to do." He grabbed it and followed the others out the door. Sandy and Lucky stayed with me, Mother Earth, and our angels.

While the others were gone, I asked, "Mother Earth, you are simultaneously at the places where you're needed, like the Divine, is that correct?"

Her voice came across like a melody of nature, "Yes, always and in all ways."

A moment later, Kyle walked through the door with everyone following him. I ran to him and threw my arms around him. His arms wrapped around me so tightly I could tell he missed me.

"I'm so glad you're back."

His hold on me tightened even more. "I'm happy as hell to be back, little princess."

That sounded odd coming from Kyle, but I realized he'd gone through hell and back. I attempted to glance around to see the others, but Kyle's hold on me kept me from moving.

"Hey, babe, we must get around the circle for the ceremony." I attempted a soft voice, but the air in my lungs seemed withheld, and I croaked my words. "You can stand beside me there." I tilted my head in the direction of the others, attempting to back out of his arms. "Kyle, we need to move now. We can talk about your experience at the mansion afterward. All right? Are you okay?" His arms continued squeezing me, and it turned into pain, like a vise. "Kyle, you're hurting me. Stop!"

He pushed me back enough that I could see his face. "Are you really pleased to see me? Show me." His eyes turned pure black momentarily, giving away my worst nightmare. Leonard had made it to this realm, now inside my husband-to-be.

I fought to get out of his arms. "Get away from me."

The others came running toward me, Lucky barking a warning. Our angels surrounded us, lifting and placing us in the circle with Leonard's Guardian Angels. The team carefully moved outside the ring, not disturbing the sea salt and lavender trail, but all the angels remained inside the circle. So did Lucky.

Kyle wouldn't let go of me, even though the angels swirled around us, touching us with tiny pinpricks of light energy that felt warm and inviting. An image of Leonard's face with pointy teeth and a slithering tongue covered Kyle's face like a misty mask. "Call off the guards and your team, or I take out Kyle for good. You know I can stop his heart."

Grams' voice went through, loud and clear, "You know what's next, Bri."

Leonard stared down at Lucky. "Well, well, who've we got here." He kicked Lucky into the air and out of the circle. I watched as his angels rescued him from falling to the floor.

Then I started, "I am filled with love and light; the Divine is my shield."

Leonard laughed like a lunatic.

I repeated the mantra, and everyone said it with me, even the angels...all of them, and I swear I heard Kyle's voice join ours. We repeated it until Kyle's body slipped to the floor, and Leonard's spirit stood beside me. I stood free of his hold, knowing he could not hurt me.

The team lit new candles and pointed them toward us. I could barely see the flames as the angels circled Kyle, Leonard, and me.

Then something else surrounded us. I could no longer see Mother Earth, but I sensed her energy. Her leafy and twining vines whirled around us. Leonard looked entrapped by that energy.

I understood to say the words: "Mother Earth calls you, Leonard Whitenmeyer. Go Now!" A crack of thunder broke the floor open, and Mother Earth's lovely face smiled at me as her vines and leaves carried a sobbing Leonard downward into the crevice.

Her calm, peaceful, mellow voice rose from the depths and said, "He will be healed and restored for his travel into the light realm, although this one might take some time for the healing. I will await his cousin, Lyndor Whitenmeyer, who I know will come willingly. Blessings." And then she faded away along with the deep crevice in the floor. Leonard's angels also vanished, but all of the others stayed.

Max, Luke, James, and Jacob entered the circle to move Kyle's body as he lay unconscious.

"Please lay him next to Lucky and my position outside the ring trail." I felt exhausted but knew the ritual needed to continue to save Lyndor and the others from the mansion.

Lucky limped over to stand beside me. "Bri, Kyle returned to the mansion to prepare the others. You can start the ceremony anytime, as I'm fairly certain they are ready for their journey."

I crouched down to pet my puppy and felt where he got kicked. I watched his Guardian Angels lay their hands on his hips, back, and legs. "Bless you for your protection, healing, and wisdom. Thank you for your presence." They all nodded and moved behind us as Lucky walked around me.

"He's all healed, Bri," Grams said. "Let's get the rest of those spirits back where they belong."

Mother Earth had been correct when she mentioned Lyndor would come willingly. He came and went in less than a minute, and his Guardian Angels left also. When I called for the Guardian Angels of all the people that resided in the mansion, the pole barn became full of angels. Those people had a lot of angels taking care of them.

One woman's spirit came forward. She announced herself as Janelle. I recalled seeing her in the top window at the mansion. "I'd like to spend time with Mother Earth if possible. I believe some of my healing must come directly from her. Can that happen?"

"Bri, if Mother Earth is open to Janelle, she'll automatically open her door. Go ahead and send Janelle." Grams enlightened me in the proper direction.

"I heard your grandmother, and thank you both for asking Mother Earth." Janelle stepped forward, away from the rest. Another spirit ran toward Janelle, and they embraced for a moment. "Anne, you'll soon be with your family. And when I get to the light realm, I'll visit you." They hugged one more time.

Anne said, "I love you like a sister. I'll never forget you, Janelle." Then Anne stepped back to join the others.

I recognized Anne's voice and realized she'd helped me at the mansion when I'd gotten captured. I nodded toward her, and she smiled. Then I said, "Mother Earth calls you, Janelle. Go Now!"

Mother Earth rose through the floor with no crack of thunder or gaping crevice. She wrapped her treelike arms around Janelle, and they disappeared, sliding into the earth below the floor.

I noticed that Kyle sat beside my feet. He'd returned, and I wanted so badly to hug him, but I knew all these people had waited so long to move into the light and see their families.

He looked up at me. "Get those people into the light realm, Bri. They need healing, and their families can do that for them."

I glanced around at our team; they all had giant smiles, which brought tears to my eyes because they all knew what came next. "Light, come now. Fill these people with your love and healing essence so they may join their families in your realm." The team and the group from the mansion repeated those words with me two more times. A warm brilliance came down through the ceiling and filled the center where the group stood, elongating like an open doorway into the bright light. Voices from the other side called to individuals in the group, and they all entered as named one by one. Once the mansion spirits had entered, the brilliance in the room disappeared along with the angels, and it ended with a tiny electric pop, verifying the ceremony had ended.

"You all may blow out your candles," I announced.

And Sandy spoke up, "Everyone takes a turn smudging the place down. We don't want any negative energy left behind."

Kyle stood and wrapped his arms around me. "I've missed you, Bri. More than ever, and there's so much to tell, and yet, I don't feel like sharing any of it."

"I get it, Kyle. You don't have to share anything at all. I'm just so happy you're back and not injured." I reciprocated and weaved my arms around him, gently kissing his warm lips. "Man, that mansion was a big case. It's going to take some time to get past it."

"Yea, I'll need to call Dad and let him know KPD Sergeant Morrison's cadaver dog, Buster, will need to run the grounds. I know many bodies of men, women, and babies are buried all around that area."

I swore my heart turned inside my chest. "That monster will not easily get forgotten. And I'm glad we could rescue everyone, which you became a big part of. You helped in their preparation on agreeing to go into the light. Your spirit traveled outside of your body and through time. That's a new experience for you."

"We can talk about that later. I need some sleep and want my partner with me for that experience." He grinned at me. "You up for that?"

"Are you?" I winked at him just as Jacob came up behind me.

"Hey, I had a thought while this amazing ceremony went down. What would you think about each of us having a hearing device with a microphone attached to it? I can give the others a play-by-play of what's happening during the ceremony. Like a picture of those angels coming in, the white light, or Mother Earth...how awesome for everyone to know in the moment about what's happening right in front of them."

Sandy and James stood close enough to hear Jacob and walked over. "I think that's a great idea—we actually have some of that equipment we use to communicate with our tech guys when out on a case. Sandy and I stay connected with them, but the team can also stay connected that way. It sounds like a great way for us to know what is happening as it happens for when we need to make a quick change or require specific equipment at that moment." James looked at Sandy. "What are your thoughts?"

"The same as yours. Jacob, that's a great idea, and it would have been wonderful tonight when all of our Guardian Angels and Mother Earth came to join in on our ceremony." Sandy smiled at me. "Bri, we'll want a full report on paper because it seems none of us thought about taping this one. None of our tech guys could make it here due to the continuous snowstorm, and James nor I realized there wasn't a camera or soundtrack rolling." She sighed. "But now we have two people who can witness everything, so maybe, Jacob, you wouldn't mind helping Bri with the reporting?" One of Sandy's brows rose as she studied Jacob.

Jacob glanced around the room as Max and Luke walked up also. "We heard you guys," Luke said. "We agree with using the equipment. It's like seeing the event through your eyes."

"That would be amazing," Max added.

Lucky gave a little bark for attention. I scooped him into my arms, and then Grams said, "Well, it sounds like you have a plan, and everyone agrees. It's time for me to return, as I promised the Divine. Tell your Gramps, I miss him and will see him on the other side. Bri, I have a message for you and Jacob, you make quite the team in more ways than you know. Stick together."

"Grams? Jacob, did you just now see anything?" I stared at Lucky, unsure why I could see all other spirits but not my grandmother's. And what did she mean by that last thing about Jacob and me?

"No, was I supposed to?" Jacob glanced around the room.

"Grams just left Lucky. She made a promise to the Divine. For whatever reason, I've never seen Grams' spirit. I wondered if you could. Did you hear the last thing she said?" I glanced at Jacob but clasped Kyle's hand as he leaned into my side. He took Lucky from me. "Do you want to write that report tonight or wait until the morning?" I asked Jacob.

But James answered, "Well, it's already morning, like almost 2:45 a.m. Let's leave the pole barn to clean up later. Everyone find a free bedroom if you don't already occupy one, upstairs or down, and then we'll figure it all out when we wake up, which very well could be noonish." James slipped his arm around Sandy. "Does that sound like a good plan?"

"Yea, I'm toast. Let's get some shut-eye. Oh, and in answer to your question, Bri, I didn't hear your grandmother." Jacob's eyes looked tired and maybe a little sad too.

I glanced at Kyle, who winked at me with maybe a little meaning behind it.

"Hey." Max and Luke stared at us with their silly grins. "You two go run your plan, and we'll run ours." Then Max and Luke headed for the door.

Whatever that meant. Kyle leaned into me and whispered, "Let's go run our plan while Max and Luke run theirs." He looked at me with his brows waggling up and down. *Okay, now I got it.*

The rest of us went to the house, with Sandy and James leaving last to shut off the lights in the pole barn.

Chapter Nineteen

Bri

I awoke too early for going to bed so late, concerned about finding the unmarked graves of all the people we sent to the light realm last night. Lucky lay fast asleep in his box. I slipped out of Kyle's arms, dressed, grabbed my toothbrush and toothpaste, and headed to the bathroom downstairs. Someone occupied it when I arrived, so I went to the couch where my laptop lay.

"Good morning." Jacob strolled out of the bathroom. "What a night, am I right? I've never witnessed angels, the doorway to Mother Earth, or the light realm. Never realized I could until last night." He stopped beside me. "Are you writing up last night's report or researching something?"

"I wondered if cadaver dogs could smell hundred-and-some-year-old bones in a grave under a few feet of snow." I glanced up at Jacob as I typed in 'Michigan Cadaver Dogs.' "You wouldn't happen to know anything about cadaver dogs, would you?"

"Funny thing...I do. My brother trains them, and it takes a lot of training time. The thing is, he lives in southern Indiana."

"Wow. Would you mind calling and asking him?" I knew about KPD Sergeant Morrison's Buster but wasn't sure about the age of the bones or the added snow.

"Calling who and asking what?" Kyle hurried down the stairs and stopped at the bottom of the stairway.

Jacob shared about his brother, Mike, and the dog training. Apparently, Mike was also an officer in the military, and the dogs were used for finding bodies in the water, on land, in avalanches, cave-ins, or mudslides. Deep snow didn't seem to matter, but he did wonder about the age of the bones, so he wanted to call and verify with Mike.

"Before you call your brother, let me give Morrison a call. We've used Buster in the past to find bones for cold cases. They may not have been over a hundred years old, but they were decades old and sometimes under snow." Kyle smiled at me and bent down to kiss my forehead. "You're looking pretty perfect this morning, woman."

"Thanks, man. You're looking pretty dapper yourself, mister." I looked around. "Where's Lucky?"

"Oops, I left him upstairs. I forgot to wake him up and take him outside. I'll take care of that right now." He glanced at Jacob. "I'll give Morrison a call in a few minutes. Don't bother your brother until I hear from Morrison, okay?"

"Sure, no worries." Jacob's stomach growled loudly. "Is there a restaurant that's close to here?"

Sandy entered from the hallway office door in time to hear Jacob. "I happen to know a place, and we all deserve a morning outing. Breakfast sounds good, and so does coffee." She walked into the kitchen to look out the window. "That sunshine will melt some of the snow, so it should make it easier to drive. There's a great restaurant just down the road, about four or five miles away. They serve the best coffee and omelets, any kind you want of either." She turned toward us with a big smile on her face. "You have no idea how happy I'm feeling today about all that went down last night. We can take care of stuff in the pole barn after we eat, or maybe we'll want to leave that set up for the rituals we perform here. I want to talk about that over breakfast."

"Sounds like a great plan." I closed my laptop as Kyle ran up the stairs to fetch Lucky.

"Jacob or Bri, would one of you want to check on Max and Luke to see if they want to join us." Sandy waited at the kitchen counter.

"Of course. I live with them, so I'll do it. They went downstairs, right?" I was so tired when we came inside last night that I never noticed anyone's room set up.

"Yep, they ended up in the first room to your right at the bottom of the steps. Tell them we can leave soon, as James is already plowing out the driveway. We heard a county plow come down the road earlier, thankfully. We started to think they'd forgotten about our road." She walked behind the counter for a cup of coffee out of an insulated carafe. She held the carafe up. "Does anyone want a cup of wake-up before we leave?"

Jacob and I raised our hands. Sandy grabbed a couple of cups from the cupboard. "Help yourselves, and I know Bri has a secret recipe for her cups." She chuckled as she pulled out the milk from the fridge.

Kyle came down the steps with Lucky attached to his leash. "I'll call Morrison while Lucky does his thing." He quickly pulled on his coat and went out the door.

Jacob walked over to the carafe while I headed down the basement stairway. The guys' bedroom door was cracked open, so I tapped on it and then entered. They were dressed and embracing each other. "Good morning, dudes."

"Hey, come on in for a snuggle." Luke held out an arm so I could step in for a hug. Max also reached out his arm as I headed over, and they enveloped me in a warm group cuddle. "You were amazing last night, Bri. Max and I talked about what went down for a long time after we went to bed. Even if we didn't see everything, we definitely felt it all. I wish we could have used some of the equipment that would have shown us some of it. Didn't think about it with the setup."

We broke apart as I glanced around the room. Those boys were always so organized. The bed had gotten made, and their suitcase had been packed.

"Hey, we're going to a restaurant Sandy recommended for breakfast a few miles down the road. Are you guys hungry?"

"We're both famished...and ready for a caffeine fix." Max immediately headed for the door.

"Well, Sandy told me the county plow came through earlier this morning, and James is now plowing the driveway. We should be ready to head out shortly." I followed Max out of the door, and Luke shut off the light and carried the suitcase, following behind me.

"We can take Jacob with us in the four-wheel drive, and you can take James and Sandy in Kyle's SUV." Max practically ran up the steps. "I smell coffee."

Sandy stood behind the counter where the pot brewed fresh coffee. "You boys want a little wake-up before we head out?"

Max went right to the cups and grabbed two. "Yep, fill us up." He chuckled.

Jacob sat at the counter, watching Max and Luke. I went over to sit beside him just as Kyle walked into the entryway with Lucky. "James just finished. He's coming inside to warm up and then will be ready to leave. He said the road looks drivable."

Lucky ran over to me, dragging his leash.

"Who's a good boy." I jumped off the bar stool and picked him up for a hug, which immediately made me think of Grams. I missed her and realized I'd never learned where she went after she left Lucky. I knew it wasn't always to the mansion. She had to recharge somewhere, but where?

"I think we should keep Lucky here in his box to sleep. He should do fine in the upstairs bedroom where he can smell us." Kyle stood beside me and patted Lucky. "He did his numbers like the grand little beast he is."

Jacob chuckled. "Hey, did you get a hold of Morrison?"

"Yea, he wants to test Buster. The temperature should be higher the next few days with sunny skies, which means melting snow. Morrison would like to see what Buster can do in this situation. The dog has never had to find bones as old as these, and Morrison thinks the challenge would be great training." Kyle took Lucky out of my arms. "I'm going to run the pup upstairs and get him situated so we can head out. I'm starving."

* * *

We sat at a corner table, quickly placing our food order. The place seemed quaint, with big windows and lots of tables and chairs, even a few booths running down one wall. Several delicious-looking baked goods were displayed underneath the cash register. After the waitress filled our cups, she brought two carafes of coffee and set them on the table, which seemed impressive. James had reminded her that everything was on his tab this morning. As I glanced around the table, everyone seemed lighthearted, smiling, possibly realizing what wonderful and thoughtful bosses James and Sandy were or happy because all the scary stuff with Leonard and the mansion was finally over.

"So, let's talk about last night. I'm sure Bri had a lot on her plate running the ceremony, so she probably didn't catch every visual thing. But what about you, Jacob? Can you share a play-by-play with us?" James glanced around the restaurant. "Maybe keep the volume low so as not to disturb those around us?" His head tilted, and one brow rose like an exclamation point to his question.

Jacob began at the start of the ritual, and his remarkable memory and point of view came across to everyone. I recalled every visual and sensitivity so much that I relived all of it, and my 'happy' faltered a few times. The count of spirits that Leonard had trapped in his loop was so many, and none of us had actual names of who these people were or where they came from, but knowing all their spirits, even the babies, rested in the Divine's light realm gave me solace. Now to find their bodies and give them a proper burial in the earth realm.

* * *

Kyle

As Jacob ran through last night's big event, I watched Bri's reactions, from smiles to jaw tension and drawn brows to half smiles. She'd been through a heinous experience with Leonard and had kept it all to herself. Now that I had my inner battle scars from Leonard and Lyndor, I understood her responses firsthand. This case was a doozy that would stick with us for a long time, maybe forever. Thank goodness Bri and I had each other to live, learn, and heal from our trauma.

Bri's hands were gripping the edges of her chair seat. I slipped my hand over hers, clasping the one on my side, then dragged it to my lap, gently squeezing her hand with both of mine. She glanced toward me and nodded, mouthing, "Thank you."

Jacob continued talking. Even after our food delivery, everyone was eating but him.

Finally, James said, "Maybe we should just all eat for now so we can get back to writing reports and cleaning up. You guys are probably chomping at the bit to get home anyway. Am I right?"

He was right, at least speaking for myself. I wanted to get Bri home and make our wedding plans. That might give her something else to think about rather than the spirits getting trapped here for such a long time. Knowing Bri, she had put herself in their place and taken on their pain and sadness. Empathy seemed the hardest to overcome of all her many gifts as she would take on anyone's emotional pain to free them from it.

* * *

Bri

When we returned to SPI Headquarters, aka James and Sandy's place, Kyle let Lucky outside to potty while Jacob and I wrote a report for the mansion haunting. I couldn't wait to get home, take a hot bath, and veg out for the rest of the day. Kyle had packed the SUV with everything, including Lucky's sleep box. Max and Luke had taken on cleaning up the pole barn with James and Sandy. They finished about the same time Jacob and I completed our report.

"I'm so grateful you are on our team, Jacob. You are the first person that can see and hear what I can. I know there are others like us, and maybe someday we'll meet more of them. But for now, thanks so much for joining SPI and becoming one of the team.

"You have no idea how much I enjoy working for James and Sandy. I appreciate your training also. I've been making notes to learn those mantras and run a ritual like you. You are so good at it."

"I can make you copies of Grams' mantras and the important parts of her journal. You should know everything by heart in case a desperate spirit comes your way. Sometimes they aren't nice spirits that lost their way to the light realm as you've personally experienced with Leonard."

Sandy walked over to the couch where we sat. "So, you've finished the report."

Jacob handed it to her. "Yea, we've been talking about training. Bri's going to give me some copies of her Grams journal pages."

"I have copies for you already made. Let me grab those, and then I think you're finished." Sandy headed toward the door to the SPI offices.

James passed her at the door and entered the house. "Hey, Max and Luke said they'd see you back at the house. And I told them we'd follow up with you after the cadaver dog finds the burial grounds. I don't mind helping however I can if needed."

Kyle came in from the entry room. "Morrison thought tomorrow might be a good day to check out the mansion grounds with Buster. It's supposed to get warmer tomorrow, and a lot of melting is happening from today's temperatures. James, I heard you mention you'd be available if needed. We have it covered, but we'll keep you informed. The police department will send out Morrison first to mark the gravesites, and then, their specialists will remove the bones, so each site's 'remains' stay together in one verified container." Kyle glanced at me. "Are you ready? Lucky's waiting in the SUV."

Jacob moved off the couch and walked over to Kyle while I packed my laptop. "Hey, thanks for everything. I'm glad you were with me at the mansion." Jacob gave Kyle a bro-hug.

And Kyle slapped him on the back of his shoulder. "I can say the same about you, Jacob. Thanks for having my back."

"So, we're actually going home." I hugged Sandy, James, and Jacob. "I'll be back here tomorrow for work."

"You're going to work from home tomorrow if there's any of that to do. Take some time, Bri, this was a pretty hefty case, and we know it had to take a lot out of you...it did to us, and we didn't really do anything." James chuckled and then shook Kyle's hand. "See you when I see you. The same goes for you regarding SPI, Kyle. No one needs to come in tomorrow. Keep me informed about the mansion burials, though."

"We will." Kyle helped me into my coat and then grabbed my laptop case. We hurried out.

"Looks like Jacob is hanging out a little longer." I noticed that he hadn't put his coat on.

"Yea. Jacob had some things he wanted to talk about with Sandy and James." Kyle started the SUV, turned the vehicle around, and drove down their long driveway. "He's a great guy and seems to fit our team well, especially nice right now while Max and Luke are involved in their careers."

"Do you know where he lives?"

"The opposite direction of us, north and west of James. Probably several miles away from the mansion. He mentioned that he'd driven a snowmobile past it, and that's when he saw the women outside it in the snow."

"Jacob seems like an intelligent man with the gift of paranormal sight and sound, and he's catching on quickly, but I don't feel like it's from my training. I believe he's done it on his own, maybe not just like me, but I sense he has rituals or ceremonies to place spirits where they need to go in the afterlife." I wasn't exactly sure when I started feeling that way, but he'd caught on so fast. "When I realized how much he could see and hear, how could he not know how to help the lost spirits?"

Chapter Twenty

Bri

"Okay, Detective Kyle Benton, I think you should do a little research on Jacob, like a background check on where he's from and what he does for a living." I stared at Kyle as he walked across our living room and settled on the couch beside me.

"Why are you tuned in on thinking that Jacob knows more than he shared with us? Why would he do that after all he and I have been through together?" Kyle leaned into me. "He's a good guy, Bri."

"I can't tell you why I sense these feelings about him. I know he's a good guy, but why would he hold on to secrets? I know he's not telling us everything he can do regarding spirits." I thought about Jacob and how he acted around all of us. He was a good guy. "It isn't an uneasy feeling, Kyle, but it's like an I-can't-put-my-finger-on-it feeling about him. Is he testing our group? SPI? Or just me? Something's a little off, and I won't rest until I get the goods on him."

"I'll see what I can find on him. Probably nothing, but I'll check for you." Kyle pulled me close and kissed me thoroughly. "We can take a nap or shower before we start our

Jacob Redding investigation." His grin spread as his brows did their smolder thing.

I took a deep breath, wanting to follow him toward either destination, yet knowing I wouldn't settle until I knew Jacob. "Not fair, nor is it funny. We need to get answers before going to the mansion again, which will probably happen tomorrow."

Kyle turned serious, lips pinching together. "Fine. I'll call Dad, and between the two of us, we'll figure out exactly the best way to find out about Jacob Redding. You stick with whatever you're doing, and I'll leave you alone."

"Would you take Lucky outside before you leave?" I blinked my eyes at him like a Betty Boop replica. I only knew about those eyes from a collection my gramps had stashed away.

"Come on, Lucky, let's go get frosty." Kyle leashed the pup, shrugged into his coat and gloves, and then headed for the door.

I sat back, still confused about my sensitivity toward Jacob, and wondered why it was intensifying. I entered his name and Kalamazoo County, MI, to see if anything came up. There were a couple of sites I could sign up to join and pay money to get information, but I would have to weed through seventy-some people. And honestly, why would those sites know anything about him? It seemed scary with personal information available to anyone that wanted to know. It should be illegal.

I felt lost and alone. I missed Grams, wishing we'd had more time to discuss our past and find out things that would help me in the future. Maybe it was time to see Gramps. Then my cell phone rang. *Luke.* "Hey, did you guys get stuck somewhere on your way home?"

"Actually, we went back to the hotel. We're headed to our culinary training shortly. Your dad put us on for late afternoon and evening under the tutelage of the greatest chef we've ever met. He's fascinating. And, for whatever reason, we hit it off with him...I mean, we might be his favorites in our class." Luke chuckled, and I heard Max join in.

"So, are you staying the night there?"

"That's why I called. I didn't want you to worry about why we didn't come home. We'll have a heavy day again tomorrow, so we decided to stay another night at the hotel."

"Makes sense. Thanks for calling because you know I would have worried. Love you, Luke. Have fun tonight with your chef. Learn lots!"

"You know me so well. Talk again soon." He hung up, and the line went dead, sinking me into the weird feeling again. Darn, I should have asked Luke if he or Max had odd feelings about Jacob.

Kyle walked in with Lucky. "He did his number one and two, so he should be good for a while. I'm heading into the office. Dad's already there. He has a woman at the station

216

who knows all the web links for a full background search. She's making me a listing of what I'll require." He had the biggest smile on his face. "Oh, also, James called me. They have another case north of us, like several hours. A ski resort has a wooded area trail for cross-country skiers and snowshoe enthusiasts, and it seems something paranormal happens there after dark, even with all the trail lights on. James wondered if we'd be interested in checking that place out in the next day or so."

"Give me the name of the resort, and I'll do some online checking, like see how long it takes to get there and maybe the lay of the wooded area."

"Great Northern Ski Resort, outside of Cadillac. It isn't a huge resort, but the place has a lot of land. They promised our business a couple of rooms to stay in while there. In the summer, they use the snow trails for horse ride trails." He stomped the snow off his boots and hurried over to kiss me goodbye. "See you later."

"Tell James that we're interested. I'll see if Gramps would mind watching Lucky for us."

"It might take a couple of days, so make sure your gramps is up to the task." Kyle toweled the snow off Lucky and then left.

I liked having something to research other than Jacob or the people that died at the mansion.

***

Kyle

As soon as I got inside the SUV on the main road to town, I used the hands-free vehicle phone system to call James. "Hey, James, I wanted to tell you that Bri is ready to head north. She's already researching the place for the lay of the land. It will take her mind off Jacob for a while."

"Have you told her about Jacob?"

"Without talking to Bri's mother, Lynn, first, I'm not sure telling Bri that Jacob is her half-brother is a good idea. Lynn should tell her. I'm not sure that Bob, her dad, knows about Jacob." I turned around in the first plowed driveway I came across to head toward Lynn's house. "I'm going to talk with Lynn right now. Bri needs to know the truth about Jacob, and if Lynn isn't aware that her son knows about her, she must also hear that."

"Sounds like a safe and good plan, Kyle. Will you be ready to head north tomorrow, or do you want to wait until Buster has a go at the mansion first?" James took a drink of something; my guess was coffee."

"I'd like to go tomorrow if that's possible. Get Bri away from here because I know it will be hard for her with all the unmarked graves they'll find. There were so many spirits. I did get a count of everyone that worked there, but that doesn't account

218

for the ones that died or were killed and replaced. Honestly, this scenario could get an award as the perfect horror story."

"You're right on the horror story, and I know you're right to keep Bri away from the mansion. I think none of us should need to go there. We can hear about the report later from your father. I'm sure reports will cross his desk that gives a body count. And, maybe it's best not to know that especially because we know they all went to the light realm, as Bri puts it." James gave a deep sigh. "This case has been the hardest for Sandy and me. We've never had that many spirits in one place before."

"I'm in Lynn's driveway. I'll talk to you later. Thanks for keeping Jacob's information away from Bri until we manage the outcome." We said our goodbyes, and I parked the SUV. Bri's grandfather had just walked out of the garage door.

"I thought I heard a vehicle roll in. How are you, Kyle? How's Bri? It's been a while since I've seen either of you." He reached out a hand and shook mine. He didn't wait for me to answer any of his questions. "Let's go get a cup of coffee. I'm ready for a wee break."

I nodded and followed him inside. "Would Lynn be available to talk with me for a minute?"

"Is something wrong with Bri?" Gramps' happy expression quickly turned drawn in, like his bushy brows.

"No, but she is part of the topic I must discuss with Lynn. Would you mind asking if she has a few minutes for me?" We hadn't seen Bri's gramps in a while, and he's one of the most influential people in her life. We should cook something and bring it over to him, Lynn, and Bob. However, Bob brings home samples from the chef's specialties for their evening meal almost every night.

Gramps shuffled down the hallway to Lynn's room, where she had her office, and knocked on the door. I heard her tell Gramps to come in. A few minutes later, Gramps and Lynn walked out.

"Hi, Kyle. Is something wrong with Bri?" She wore a similar look of concern that Gramps had only moments earlier.

I looked from Lynn to Gramps and back to Lynn. "What I have to say might be a delicate subject for you, Lynn. Maybe we should chat in your office."

Gramps stepped back with his lips pinched together. When I didn't say more, he said, "I'll grab both of you a fresh cup of coffee when it's finished brewing." He waved us passed him. "I'll knock before I enter."

Once inside her room, she directed me to the chair in front of her desk. Then she settled into her chair. "Okay, Kyle. Is Bri pregnant?"

I knew my eyes popped wide open because she stunned me. I chuckled for a moment and gathered my wits. "Someone new started working at SPI. None of us knew that he had a secret agenda to meet Bri. He has the same paranormal abilities as Bri. He shared with James and me that you are listed on his adoption paperwork as his birth mother." I waited to see her response.

She tilted her head back, closed her eyes, and sighed deeply, almost as if a huge weight had just released from her chest. She stayed silent for a few moments, and so did I. After another sigh, she opened her eyes and sat straight in her chair. "Yes, I had a son. Is he called Jacob? I named him before I gave him up for adoption."

I nodded. "Yes, Jacob is his name."

"I'd like to explain why I had to give him up." She rolled her chair to the desk and folded her hands on the desktop. "First, has he said anything to Bri?"

"No, he wanted to give you a chance to explain it to her before introducing himself as her half-brother."

"That's very generous of him." She took a breath, obviously not wanting to continue, but did anyway. "I was beaten and raped when I was fifteen. Most of the bruises were on my arms and legs, and thankfully, he'd left my face alone. Dad and Mom didn't know about it for a while because it happened in the summertime, during the time I had gone and stayed at my friend's house for a month. My friend and I were afraid that if my parents found out, they would ban me from ever seeing my friend again. So, I kept it a secret.

"I didn't realize I was pregnant until four months along. I knew something had changed with my menstrual cycles, but I didn't want Dad or Mom to worry, so I never told them anything that had happened. When Mom realized that I was pregnant, she and I moved to Upper Michigan so I could keep my secret and have the baby there. Dad continued working in Southern Michigan and sending us money.

"I had come to terms, knowing I would have to give up the baby. Mom might have kept the baby, but Dad thought it best for the babe to have adoptive parents, a couple that couldn't get pregnant but wanted a baby." A tear rolled down Lynn's cheek, and she swiped it away. "I never thought I'd see Jacob again."

"Lynn, Bri has strange feelings about Jacob, like she knows something is different about him. He's a great guy, and she thinks he is also, and yet, she knows something is off with him. I believe it's because he's her half-brother. Bri wants to learn more about Jacob's background and do a deep dive into research."

Her mouth dropped open for a moment. "So, I need to tell her my secret before she finds out. That's why you're here." Lynn rolled the chair back so she could stand. "Well, Dad already knows about Jacob. I'm sure he'd like to meet him, as would I." Another tear spilled down her face, followed by a few more. She grabbed a tissue and wiped them off. "Kyle, would you mind bringing Bri here? I'd like her to spend time with Dad and me while we tell her about Jacob." She walked to the door, waved me through, then followed me to the kitchen and Gramps, who had kept the coffee cups on the counter.

"I thought you might want your coffee out here instead of in that office."

"Are you sure you didn't stop a moment outside the door to listen in?" Lynn smiled at her father, and his reaction proved her question right.

"I'll head back to the house and get Bri. She wants to introduce you to our newest family member, Lucky, a rescue puppy." I headed toward the door, but Lynn stopped me.

She hugged me. "Thank you for not judging me and for allowing me to talk with Bri before Jacob sprang his secret to her. I think this afternoon might get trying at times, but it will also clear our family from the cobwebs that have collected."

"Spoken like a true writer." I smiled and headed out.

Gramps followed me out the door. "Make sure Bri brings the pup. I think it will help to have a little distraction from what Bri will learn about her mom's history."

"Honestly, Gramps, it's not a bad thing. And my guess is everyone will get along with Jacob. He's one of the good guys."

Gramps nodded his head. "Thanks, Kyle."

On the drive to the house, I gave Dad a quick call to explain why he wouldn't see me at the police station today.

Now to pick up Bri and Lucky, take them to her moms, and possibly hang out to help keep the story straight for my wife-to-be.

Chapter Twenty-One

Bri

It startled me when the backdoor banged open. I jumped off the couch, set the laptop down, and chased after Lucky as he ran toward the door, which was something new for the pup.

Kyle stood there with a giant smile, patting Lucky's head. "Hey, I stopped by your mom's on the way to work, and stuff came up we should talk about. So, here I am, taking you and Lucky there. Your gramps wants to meet the newest addition to our family."

"Seriously? I've barely started researching the Great Northern Ski Resort. We can put the visit to Mom's off for a few days, don't you think? Besides, Mom is always busy editing. She most likely doesn't have time right now, anyway." I turned to walk back to the couch.

"No, it can't wait. Your mom has something important to tell you, and she asked me to drive you over there now." Kyle made it sound ominous, implying something might be medically wrong. "Bri, it's something you need to hear from your mom."

"So, you tell me." I waited in the doorway to the living room while he stood at the garage entry door.

Kyle's jaw tensed. "Your mother has something to tell you; you must hear it from her. She's waiting for you. I'll take Lucky out to the car."

Wow, that seemed a little harsh for Kyle. What the heck was that all about? I stood there for a few hot seconds after he shut the door. I walked to the couch to close my laptop, grabbed my coat, and slipped it on as I headed out the door. Kyle looked angry or frustrated when I climbed into the SUV. "Are you okay? Did you get some bad news or something?"

"No, just an odd day. Stuff is happening that I can't control, and sometimes it's tough to roll with the flow." He chuckled, so I guessed it might not be as bad as I thought.

"So, did you get a chance to tell James I wanted to go north?" I settled back in the seat and buckled my safety belt.

"Yes, and we can leave first thing in the morning if you want. According to the weather app, the roads should be clear most of the way. Not quite sure about the Cadillac area." Kyle pulled around the corner on the road to Mom's.

"So, it's a good thing Gramps gets to meet Lucky, and hopefully, Gramps falls for our pup like we did." I studied Kyle. He still looked upset. "Can't you give me a hint of what Mom will tell me? Aren't we a team?"

He pulled into Mom's driveway and parked near the porch. "She needs to tell you." He sighed a big breath, then looked at me. "It isn't anything bad, Bri. Things will fall together for you once you hear what she says."

"Well, that's not helpful, but okay. Let's get this over with." I jumped out of the SUV and then grabbed Lucky. "I'll carry him so he's not all snowy."

Kyle walked around the SUV to me and took the leash off Lucky's collar.

Gramps stood at the door with a big smile on his face. He opened it and waved us inside. "Who do we have here?"

"This is Lucky." I noticed the pup's interest stayed on Gramps.

Gramps lifted Lucky out of my hands, and our pup didn't seem to mind. He ruffled the fur around Lucky's ears. "Look at this handsome fella."

Mom walked over. "Thanks for coming on such short notice, Bri. I appreciate it. Here, let me take your coat." She helped me out of it, which seemed unusual.

Kyle hung up his coat and wandered over to Gramps and Lucky.

"Kyle wouldn't share anything, only that you had something important to share with me." Mom grabbed my hand and led me into the sunroom. We passed the guys occupied with the puppy on the way.

Mom shut the folding doors, so we had the room to ourselves, which frightened me about what Mom had to share.

"Please tell me your health is good. Is Dad's?" My concern blew in all kinds of directions.

She shook her head. "Bri, this is about something that happened to me when I was fifteen. I never told you, but I did tell your father years ago...just before our break-up time. I'm not sure why I didn't share this with you once you were old enough to hear it, but now I understand you must know."

A lump had formed in my throat, choking off any words that might have helped make it easier for Mom. I sat in silence and waited.

"I had just turned fifteen, staying at my friend, Sarah, and her parent's lake house for a month. We went to a beach party several doors down one night, and I met a boy I'd thought was our age. I found out later that he had graduated high school the year before. After dark, a group of us walked into the forest across the street. The boy, named Ray, pulled me aside, and we headed off in a different direction."

Mom continued the story, telling me once they got a distance away, he taped her mouth, beat her into submission, and then raped her. Ray had left her there. Mom had dressed, returned to Sarah's, and hid outside because her clothes were bloody, tattered, and torn.

"Sarah found me, and we snuck in, making it to the bedroom without getting caught. Sarah helped me recover without telling her parents or my parents. Then when I went home, I never said anything to my parents...until they discovered I was four months pregnant."

Mom's story broke my heart. I can't imagine all that she'd been through and that Grams moved away with her so Mom could have the baby and give him up for adoption. They had a story that kept it all under wraps to the neighborhood, and it sounded like Sarah kept the secret also, which made me want to meet this woman.

"Bri, I understand the baby I had is someone you know and I've yet to meet. His name is Jacob Redding."

My mouth dropped open as my brain went into backup mode. No words came, only thoughts of Jacob, how we met and worked together, his paranormal gifts, and my training him when he already knew everything. It suddenly all made sense...and my sensitivities toward him...why I resonated with him. Oh. My. Gods!

I looked at Mom as her eyes filled and overflowed.

"Say something, dear Bri." Mom stood in the middle of the room. Her body trembled.

I saw the fear in her eyes that I wouldn't understand, but I did. I jumped off the chair and ran to her, wrapping my arms around her. "Mom, I love you. I understand, and I'm so sorry that happened to you."

"Oh, my heavens, I was so afraid you would hate me for not telling you." Mom's arms tightened around me. "I love you, too."

I moved away just enough to see her face, and she studied mine. "Mom, that means I am not an only child. I have a half-brother, Jacob." I went in for another hug. "I'm so grateful you told me and that I've already met Jacob. It's like the synchronicity came into play and lined up for us, like stars in the sky, to meet our relative, your son and my brother. Mom, that's amazing. You're going to fall in love with Jacob." My heart pumped over time with the thrill of what I had just learned, and then I remembered what Grams said about Jacob and me, how we made such a good team. She had known Jacob was my half-brother.

When we left the room, Kyle, Gramps, and Lucky all stared at us, and then the doorbell rang. Kyle's body straightened, and his lips pressed together for a second. He looked toward the door and back at us. "I called Jacob to come and meet you, Lynn."

Mom's eyes filled with tears again, and she choked out, "I'm ready. Open the door."

* * *

Kyle

I walked out the door and shut it.

230

Jacob tilted his head, "I thought you told me to come and meet my mother. Did she change her mind?"

"No, she's ready to meet you. Bri's happy to find out the sensitivities she has felt about you has been answered. She knows that you're her half-brother."

"Then why are we still standing out here?" Jacob nodded his head with a giant smile on his face.

"Only preparing you for a good reception. Hope you can handle it." I opened the door, and everyone rushed over and gave Jacob a group hug. Even I jumped in on that one.

Everyone started talking at the same time until suddenly laughter filled the room.

"I'm going to fix us a pizza to celebrate, and you'll help me, Kyle." Bri grabbed my hand. "I think it's Gramps, Mom, and Jacob's turn to take that sunroom over." Bri nodded toward the others, and they headed into the sunroom.

I hadn't seen Bri look this happy in a long time. She sometimes carried the weight of the world with her empathic and compassionate abilities; seeing her weightless from it was my personal gift. Right then, I decided we should include Jacob in our trip north because whatever haunted the forest might require more than Bri and me. Jacob could see and hear what Bri does, and I could run the equipment. If he wanted to ride with us, everything would fit inside the SUV, even Jacob.

"Hey, what would you say to Jacob coming with us on the northern trip tomorrow? I'd feel better having one more person with us. Jacob can see and hear what you do, so he'd be the perfect extra to take. What do you think?" I washed my hands and grabbed the shortening and two pizza pans to grease for the dough Bri pounded and stretched.

"That's a great idea. We probably won't get a very early start, though, because we'll need to grab some equipment from SPI, and Jacob will need to get whatever he needs to come with us." She threw the dough into a bowl and covered it with a towel. "This is going to take about five minutes. I'm going to cut up the pepperoni and shred the cheese." She pulled out some pizza sauce and a can of mushrooms Lynn had in the cupboard, grabbed the other stuff out of the fridge, and the shredder, pizza cutter, and knife from a drawer.

"Dang, girl, you should have been a chef." I poked her in the side. "I can cut the pepperoni, and you shred the cheese."

* * *

The pizzas got devoured in less than twenty minutes, and everyone appeared satisfied. Jacob sat next to Lynn at the counter, both appearing happy. "Hey, Jacob, would you consider going north with Bri and me tomorrow for a new SPI case?"

He grinned at me. "James told me about it, and I volunteered to go along. I thought I'd have to drive separately."

Bri walked up right then. "Nope, we'd like you to ride with us, but we figured you'd have to go home and do some packing. We can wait for you, though."

"I brought my bag of clothes, and James asked me to take some recording equipment. Sandy gave me some protection stuff and everything it takes to make a ritual circle if the need arises. It's in my truck. When you called me, I was on my way into town from SPI." Jacob took a drink of his cola and then glanced around the room. "This day...it's the best I've had in a long time."

"We have an extra bedroom at our house. Why don't you stay the night, and then we can leave after breakfast." Bri had that festive look she got when expecting an affirmative response.

"Sure. If it's all right with you, Kyle, that'll work."

"Yes, you can stay with us, bro."

Chapter Twenty-Two

Bri

I woke up first while Kyle slept soundly. I climbed out of bed and quickly dressed. Lucky hunkered down in his box, not ready to rise and shine. So, I headed to the kitchen to get some coffee brewing and make breakfast, but the aroma of fresh coffee wafted through the living room before I reached my destination.

"Good morning, sunshine." Jacob stood up from the couch with a cup of coffee in hand.

"How did I miss you on my way by?"

"Your eyes were closed. I think you were smelling my coffee." He waggled his brows. "Want some?"

"You made coffee? Yes, I want some. I was just going to start breakfast." I turned toward the kitchen.

"Wait, I have a better suggestion."

I looked back at Jacob. "Okay, out with it."

"Let's stop somewhere on our way north for breakfast. I'm not that hungry." He followed me toward the coffee pot.

I poured a little into my cup, topped off his, and filled most of mine with milk. "I think that's a great idea. I'm not hungry either, probably because we ate late at Mom's place." I stuck my cup in the microwave for a minute. "So, we never asked you about your meeting with Mom and Gramps. Did everything go all right?"

"How could it not? Our Mom is genuine, honest, and seems like a caring soul. Gramps has a hilarious sense of humor. Both made me feel comfortable and Mom's story about how I happened into her world, well, let's just say I'm happy I didn't get aborted." He settled against the other side of the middle countertop.

"How old are you anyway?" I thought he looked close to Kyle and my age.

"I'm thirty-one, and you're twenty-four, the same age as Kyle, right?"

"We both turned twenty-five in December. Our birthdays are close together. So, you are six years older, and honestly, you look the same age as us."

"Hey, you better have left some coffee for me." Kyle wandered over and grabbed a cup out of the cupboard. "What are we talking about?" He filled his cup and topped off Jacob's and mine.

"We decided to eat on the road after dropping Lucky off with Gramps. Where is our boy?" I glanced behind him to see if Lucky followed.

"Still sleeping. What a sleepy head." Kyle chuckled. "I can bag Lucky's stuff for Gramps and bring the sleep box. I'm glad those two hit it off. Gramps looked excited about having Lucky."

"Yeah, I got that feeling also." Jacob stepped over to look out the window. "Not snowing now, and no new snow, plus there's water dripping off the awning. Bring your sunglasses. It looks like it'll get reflective for driving."

"I'll wake Lucky and grab his stuff. We can take the same suitcase as we took to SPI because it's still packed. I'll carry that out also." He stopped beside Jacob a moment. "Do you want to load the SPI equipment into the SUV? I can help if it's heavy. We might as well get loaded and go." Kyle glanced at the clock. "Yea, we'll have a nice start and probably get there right after lunchtime."

Both guys headed off, and I finished my coffee and turned off the pot. Lucky's leash hung on a hook by the door, so I grabbed that to let him out. Kyle was stacking stuff on the bed when I walked into the bedroom. Lucky jumped around like a little crazy head. "This boy has to go." I hooked him up, leaving Kyle to pack. Everything I needed was already in the suitcase.

I met Jacob on the way outside. "Lucky's crossing his legs. Gotta move." We both laughed at the crazy puppy. Jacob headed to the front, where he parked his truck, and Lucky and I went out the backside of the garage for him to go potty. When Lucky and I came inside, the overhead garage door opened, and Kyle backed the SUV outside.

They must have already loaded it with the equipment because Jacob drove his truck inside the garage.

With Lucky following me, I ran into the house to get my laptop, purse, cell phone...and a pair of sunglasses. I grabbed Kyle's sunglasses off our dresser. The guys were already inside the SUV when I came out. I loaded Lucky, ran back to the garage door, and locked it. The back door to our garage always remained locked from the outside.

When we got to Mom's, Gramps stood by the door when Kyle and I entered with Lucky. The pup went into an excited frenzy to see Gramps. So cute. The two of them had fallen for each other. I walked over to Gramps and hugged him. "Thank you for watching over our Lucky. He's lucky to have you, Gramps...just like me."

"Oh, Snickers, don't be funnin' with me."

"I'm not. Oh, there is something I neglected to tell you last night, probably because my head was preoccupied with whatever Mom had to tell me." I chuckled, and so did he. "I have a message from Grams to you. She said that she loves and misses you and will be waiting for you on the other side. And there's no hurry...she has eternity to wait."

"Was Ileana here? In the earth realm?" Gramps snuggled Lucky in his arms, and the dog calmed right down.

"She helped us with our last case. Thank goodness for her. We really needed her. She hung out inside Lucky for a while...maybe that's why Lucky acts like he knows you already."

Gramps looked down at Lucky and patted the pup's head. "I thought there was something familiar about this little guy." He chuckled again.

"I never saw Grams as a spirit, but I could always hear her voice. I'm not sure why that happened when I can see all other spirits."

"I'm sure there's a good reason for it, Snickers. You need to get going before your ride leaves you stranded." Gramps walked me to the door, and we hugged again, even with Lucky still in his arms.

Those two would have a ball while Kyle and I were away.

* * *

The drive to Cadillac seemed fast, maybe because we talked all the way and even forgot to stop and eat. The Great Northern Ski Resort looked amazing from the outside and even more so on the inside with wooden shellacked walls and floors, tables and chairs, lamps, and picture frames, looking rustic but so beautifully nature-rich. And the main floor had a huge stone fireplace with a massive wooden mantel, showing off the snapping, vibrant log fire piled on a large cast iron grate. Couches and chairs made a semi-circle around it, and a few people sat there, reading or watching the blazing fire.

The place had extra large windows, showing off the snowy hills, the skiers, and the snowboarders. Then I peeked into another room off the main one and found a restaurant. I picked up a menu, and they served three meals daily and alcoholic beverages. And I noticed some people sitting at a bar on one end of the room, enjoying an even better view of the snowy wonderland of people outside enjoying themselves.

Jacob startled me from behind. "Hey, would you like to eat before we go to our rooms? Someone can take our luggage to the rooms so we can settle right here if you'd like."

Kyle came in a moment later, stunned by the room like I was. "Well, where should we sit? I'm famished, and a large cola sounds good. The manager we talked with had a guy take the luggage to our rooms."

Jacob led us to a table by a window. "This isn't too bright for you, is it?"

"It's gotten cloudy since we arrived. Like the sun took a nap for a bit." I giggled as a waitress dropped three menus on the table.

"What would you all like to drink?" She pulled out a small tablet and held a pen at the ready. She rattled off a few favorites, and I chose an iced tea. The guys picked large colas. "Are these going to be separate bills?" She glanced around the table.

Kyle turned away from the window to look at the waitress. "One tab, mine." When she walked away, Kyle added, "James said SPI covers our meals and the rooms if they charge us. I carry one of their credit cards."

The waitress carried our drinks over and took our food orders. We all ordered different sandwiches with homemade chips and coleslaw. We didn't talk much until we finished, and then Kyle wanted to check the area where their haunting issue had happened.

"I think we should check with the owner here and get the full details of what happened. We'd have a better idea of what to take out there. Plus, we need directions on where we're going." I sounded full of it, like a bossy pants, but those were my thoughts on a plan of action. And it got dark pretty quickly at this time of the year.

"Yea, you're right. I'll take care of the bill, and you and Jacob find the resort manager. He can show us the trail and maybe give us an idea of how long it takes to get there. And do we have to use snowshoes or cross-country skis?"

Jacob added, "Or snowmobiles?"

Kyle nodded. "A couple of snowmobiles with a sled behind them for our equipment would be perfect."

I agreed. "Let's go find the management, Jacob."

* * *

We ended up on snowmobiles, and they did have sleds we could use for our equipment. Finding the spot where a couple heard more than one person moaning, like people hurt or dying, took about twenty minutes. They also heard terrifying screaming and consistent running, like someone running to escape. But the day after the incident, when the police and ski rangers came out to look the area over, the only prints in the snow were those of the couple's snowshoes.

A trail patrolman guided us to the specific spot. We stopped and got off the snowmobiles, and he led us through the trees, where the couple heard the sounds. The resort had closed off this trail until we figured out what had created the event. Apparently, that couple was one of many to have witnessed it.

Before the trail patrolman left us, he mentioned that these weird happenings were between 10:00 p.m. and 2:00 a.m.

I wandered around while Kyle and Jacob set up some of the electronics that didn't require electricity, as a loud generator wouldn't work for us out here. Kyle had some goggles that showed different colors for paranormal energy. Jacob and I didn't require those. They also had a recorder

241

recording different frequencies that sometimes would form words. Kyle wore that strapped to his chest.

I didn't see anything out of the ordinary or feel sensitivities like usual if spirits were near. "Are we just going to hang out here and wait until 2:00 a.m.?"

Jacob walked over to an open spot between the trees. "We should hear sounds from this distance if you want to build a campfire. It looks like they have them here, as there's a stack of campfire wood. Let's pull the sleds over for seats so we're not sitting on the snow."

Jacob and Kyle went to work building the campfire from the wood and sticks while I dragged a sled over. When I pulled the second sled over, Jacob lit a torch-like lighter to start the fire. I clapped when the flame caught, and a snappy campfire ensued. We all sat and talked low so that we could hear anything unusual. The full moon brightened the night until a giant cloud skidded to a stop in front of it.

Then the first moan happened. We all perked up. I stood waiting to see a spirit, and so did Jacob. Kyle pointed the microphone toward the sound.

"Let's walk over there." I glanced at Kyle and Jacob, and both nodded in confirmation. We headed toward the sounds, now more than one moan. We came to a small clearing, and I stopped. The guys moved to each side of me.

"Oh. My. Gods," whispered Jacob. "How many do you count? They look like they are dying of cold and starvation."

Then a woman ran toward the group lying on the ground and screamed, "Where's my baby? Where's Charlie?" She looked cold and skinny but more alive than the people lying together on top of the snow as she circled them. All of them wore tattered clothing fashioned from several hundred years ago. I couldn't imagine who they were or where they were going, but I would research it when we finished.

"I don't think a ritual circle is necessary for this group. But we need to use our white tapers, light them, and point them at the people once we get evenly spaced around them. I'll start the protection mantra, and you'll repeat it with me."

We moved and positioned ourselves with enough space between the group and us for the woman circling to continue her path without blowing through us.

I looked toward the sky and placed my left hand over my heart. "I am filled with love and light; the Divine is my shield," I repeated with Jacob and Kyle three times.

Then I lit my white taper candle and pointed it toward the people in the center, and so did Kyle and Jacob. "Guardian Angels of the people here, come now. Thank you for your protection and guidance." I repeated it three times, and Jacob and Kyle joined in also. I watched as a crowd of shimmering bodies surrounded all of us. Once they moved around their person, I continued, "Light, come now. Fill these people with your love and healing essence so they may join their families in your realm."

A warm, brilliant sparkling light slid down from the sky into the center of the people lying on the ground. It elongated like a door and opened into greater brightness. Voices called to the people scattered across the snow, and one by one, each person stood and walked toward the doorway with the help of their guardian angels, who supported their fragile bodies as they crossed over. Even the woman circling, looking for her child and husband, had the help of her guardian angels as they guided her into the light realm.

I was fascinated by watching those people heal completely as they entered, finding their families, and moving onward to the beyond. My whole heart warmed, knowing I would never die alone, and there indeed was a beyond. I couldn't wait to give Kyle the details of what had happened.

After the light had folded into itself, I stood there momentarily, watching the cloud let go of the moon.

Jacob rushed over and hugged me. "I can't believe how easily you helped these spirits find the light realm. You open the door for them." He seemed breathless.

"No, I simply call upon their guardian angels and the light realm, and they help them heal and cross over. I thought you did the same thing, Jacob." I probably shouldn't have said that, but I sensed that my training for him was repeating what he already knew.

"Maybe, some of it is similar to what I do, but you have such power." He stared at me like...well, like I wasn't real.

"Okay, stop giving Bri a big head. She won't be able to walk through the doorway into the resort." Kyle walked over.

I punched him in the shoulder. "You know the entry doorway is a double door, right?"

"Yes. Are you feeling top-heavy right now?" He took off running back toward the campfire, which only had a few embers left. "Come here. I need something."

"Oh, you'll get something." I ran toward him. "My big head in your gut."

Kyle stopped me from ramming into him, but that still knocked him off his feet. He fell into a nice pile of snow, laughing in a way that sounded like all the pent-up negative energy from the mansion case came tumbling out in a contagious, giddy release. Jacob joined us, laughing his face off, and how could I not join in, so much that tears rolled down my face. If anyone listened, they'd think we lost our marbles or became drunk on "happy."

Finally, the laughter turned into giggles and then smiles. "Do you know what time it is?" Kyle stood up and brushed the snow off. "It's got to be close to midnight."

Jacob pulled out his cell phone to check. "Yep, about ten minutes after. I'd say we had a full day. I'm ready to head back and get some shut-eye."

We packed the sleds and rode the snowmobiles back, seeing a few deer scampering out of our way or owls flying through the trees. The resort had left its lights on, almost like soft daylight reflecting off the glistening snow. The air was so pure and cold that a misty fog escaped whenever we talked or let a big breath go airborne.

We decided to load the equipment into the SUV before we went to our rooms, less to pack in the morning.

"Do you think we should stay one more night to make sure all the spirits crossed over?" Jacob stood in the hallway next to his room door. "I'm thinking that if we don't, there's a possibility we'll get called right back."

I didn't think anyone got left behind, so I wondered if Jacob simply needed a break from all that went down the past few days. The mansion turned into an unsettling event, and another day away might keep us from hearing the gory details of the burial sites.

"Maybe we should talk to James in the morning and see how he feels about us taking another night to ensure our case is all wrapped up." Kyle glanced at me and then at Jacob. "Sleep in if you need to, Jacob. We probably will, and I'll give James a call. He'll want a report over the phone anyway."

"Sounds good. Night, sleep well." Jacob unlocked his door with a keycard and disappeared inside.

Kyle unlocked our door, and I couldn't wait to snuggle under the covers. Cold and tiredness would probably keep me awake for a little while...and the fact that I wanted to find out about the people who crossed into the light realm tonight.

"We should probably alert the police here. I'm betting bones are buried at the site and should get handled like at the mansion." I pulled off my winter gear and hung everything to dry.

"I'll also call Dad in the morning. He can alert the police department here without sounding like heebie jeebie. Dad will want to do a little research to sound more informative. Most departments don't believe in supernatural events. Without finding any bones or a burial site, it could sound ridiculous. And without the proper equipment to look for the bones, we have no proof."

"Yea, you're right. Those people could have been found and buried somewhere else...although I thought their spirits always stayed close to their remains." That would've been an excellent question to ask Grams.

Epilogue

Bri

We stayed two more nights at the resort, as James suggested. I believed he wanted us away from the mansion grounds investigation with Buster, the cadaver dog. I knew James and Miles (Kyle's dad) kept Kyle and Jacob updated, and I didn't mind not knowing all the details. Every spirit had left the earth realm, moving on to wherever they should, and I was at peace with it.

Jacob coming into my life seemed like a miracle blessing. I think he felt the same. And Gramps, Mom, and Dad accepted Jacob as part of our family. We discovered he had a new interest in a woman, Helena, and we met her. They were a perfect match. We also found out he knew her through a private investigative business owned by his adoptive father. Little did we know, Jacob was also a private investigator.

Lucky, our sweet boy, decided to stay with Gramps, which stirred my heart in different directions. But all in all, Lucky seemed meant for Gramps and visa-versa.

Luke and Max created fabulous dishes for us to eat almost every evening. They loved their job and mentor chef, who they invited to the house one night to blow us away with another delicious meal. I couldn't believe the resemblance between Chef Bernard Reynolds and Luke, nor how well they got along. Their wit and even their voices sounded the same, and the sensitivities I had made me wonder...

So, today, Kyle ended up driving to the police station as he had another investigation case.

I went to SPI. The roads had pretty much cleared from the sunshine and warmer temperatures. More snow was in the forecast, but that was Michigan weather. I never minded our four seasons. I had a few reports to fill out for the resort case and some accounting work to catch up on. Sandy had mentioned that she wanted to do a supply inventory also. I would stay busy for at least a week...or until another case fell into my lap.

The End

Dear Reader, Reviews mean everything to an author. They determine the placement of the book, and thus how many potential readers will see the book. I will be so grateful if you will take a minute of your time and return to the site where you purchased this book to leave a review, even just a two-line review. It doesn't matter how long, just that the book is reviewed and rated. Thank you so much for reading my book, and I hope you enjoyed it. Susan

Kendra Spark Series: Kendra sees ghosts, and then her BFF, Jenna, becomes one. The two friends and FBI agent Derek Knight fight for justice to the victims of heinous crimes. But sometimes, those crimes lead to the supernatural...

Unorthodox, **Book 1**

Malevolent, **Book 2**

Albatross, **Book 3**

Oblivious, **Book 4**

Stand Alone Paranormal, Suspense, Romance Novels:

Amber Eyes Glow

New Paranormal, Suspense, Romance Series:

Ghost Guardians, Ghost Guardian Series, Book 1

S. Peters-Davis writes multi-genre stories but loves penning a good page-turning suspense-thriller, especially when it's a ghost story *and* a romance. Paranormal suspense-thriller romances are her favorites. When she's not writing, editing, or reading, she's hiking, RV'ing, fishing, playing with grandchildren and her dog, Sparky, or enjoying time with her favorite muse (her husband) in Southwest Michigan.

BWL Publishing

bwlpublishing.ca